MW01137583

DIMENSION LAPSE
By
Nicholas T. Davis

To Brian,
My nephew who
watched the old "Planet of Apes."
This story will remind
of you of it!
Your uncle,
Nicholas T. Davis

© Copyright 2014 By Nicholas T. Davis
All Rights Reserved
ISBN: 1499366817
ISBN 13: 978-1499366815
Syracuse, NY

<u>DEDICATION</u>
This tale is dedicated to my two sisters
Cynthia Richman and Phyllis Antos
who shared my love for science fiction.

CHAPTER ONE

Jeff could still remember the exact date of his arrival on the peculiar world. It was December 15th, 2159 when he had left Pluto. He was investigating the possibility of an alien race when his instruments were damaged. His ship took a lot of beating, and it landed on a tropical island of an uncharted planet. Upon landing there, he was greeted by amphibian-like beings, which were peaceful and very primitive, living in caves prior to his arrival. They treated his wounds and helped salvage his ship. In return, Jeff helped them build homes to live in. Their mutual friendship, however, was only a substitute for human companionship.

The most outspoken alien called himself Dormiton and wasn't very large, strong or even intelligent. None of their race possessed these qualities. Even though they had human emotions, most of their decisions were logical choices. They didn't need much sleep, only three to four hours daily. Although they were smaller than humans, they still possessed similar organs, like any other amphibian would. Their lungs were a little larger in comparison due to their slightly more concentrated atmosphere, but their other organs were identical.

Dormiton was a rather inquisitive creature who was interested in where Jeff came from and who is really was. Jeff taught him everything he knew about space travel, Mars and Earth. He explained how in the year 2015 a global war almost destroyed everything on his grandparent's home planet, Earth. The survivors repaired what was left, and reached for the stars, building a space station that housed five thousand people. Their own world obliterated, they had no choice but to go to Mars to begin a massive colonization effort. Setting up huge solar panels to collect heat from the sun, they constructed a huge vegetation project. Collecting carbon dioxide from the atmosphere, sunlight from the solar panels, and water from under the soil, they were able to increase the surface temperature twenty five degrees around the biodomes, and the oxygen and nitrogen in the atmosphere by 10%. The biggest problem was little protection from gamma rays and solar radiation other than the polyethylene shielding the biodomes were coated with. It was not a perfect situation, but it allowed the air and space suits to be a little more comfortable and flexible.

Jeff was assigned to the Mars base his entire life, and never saw the Rocky Mountains of Earth, or the sandy beaches of the tropics. He only saw pictures of the way Earth used to look. Mars, for the most part was flat, rocky terrain except for Olympus Mons, Arsia Mons and the other mountains; and forests, crop fields, and lakes inside the biodome vegetation complexes. The Earth stations Edronomis and Tianos were transported away from the Earth to orbit Mars. The population before Jeff's father left the orbit of Earth had grown to 90,000 people. There were 60,000 at the Martian base where Jeff was from. He was sent on many flight missions, including retrieving ice samples from the dwarf planet Pluto.

This was his first encounter with extraterrestrials, and the last time he would see any humans for a long time. While maneuvering by Pluto, Jeff noticed a flashing light at the corner of his eye. It disappeared rather abrupt, and then reappeared minutes later, passing right by his craft. The speed of the phenomenon was far beyond Martian technology, so Jeff decided not to pursue it.

Two hours later, he made a landing on the cold, icy plains of the barren world. The solar wind was not as calm as he hoped it would be, and touchdown was a bit turbulent, but would suffice. He shut off the power supply, suited up, turned on the button of his suit's temperature control to 70°, grabbed his laser gun along with some soil sample containers and opened the main door lock. A sense of strange uneasiness came over his mind he never felt before, ghostly uneasiness, being exposed to the cold silent and raw elements of the hostile world.

He leaped gently onto the icy surface, his boots biting into it. Although none of several stories of ships that were attacked by aliens were officially substantiated, he was being cautious after hearing about them. He realized there wasn't any immediate danger, fired his laser into the ground, and melted a chunk of the frozen Nitrogen-Methane ice cover that probably had been there for thousands of years, and placed a small sample inside one of the receptacles he brought.

"Major Walker to base," he said through a transmitter in his helmet. The response was a little delayed due to the distance between worlds.

"This is Mars base," a woman's voice answered. It was Lori Anderson, a close friend and coworker, and Jeff had a fancy for her beautiful blue eyes, long blonde curly hair and ivory fair complexion.

"Have you received the soil samples yet? "Over."

"Yes," he said. "Before landing, however, I saw some kind of light in the sky. It was faster than any of our ships. I think it was a meteor, but I can't be positive."

"We'll send a couple of scouts your way," Lori answered, in a firm commanding voice. "If you're through there, Commander Carver wants you back here."

"Roger. Over and out."

Jeff retrieved the rest of his samples and headed back to the ship. Pluto was at perihelion, the closest point to the sun, and the Nitrogen-Methane was melting; a good time to drill ice cores. He was almost to the door, when the light appeared again, this time not more than ten miles away from him. He barely saw the faint beacon through the foggy, snow covered atmosphere. There were three green lights on top of a red light, and it was spherical in its black, oval shape. It came in close view, and he was convinced that it was alien. He held his laser tight, headed

6

quick back to the ship, threw his hand held core drill into the ship, climbed in, and slammed the hatch tight behind him. He turned on the power immediately, but it went dead when the alien ship fired upon him. He tried to reach Mars base, but couldn't establish any radio contact. Beginning to panic, he grabbed his laser pistol and some explosives and headed for the escape hatch below the ship. He heard the sound of lasers as they blazed against the main door hatch. He pushed the escape door hatch open and gently dropped to the ground below the ship.

He could see his aggressors as he peered from the corner of one of the landing pods. He saw two of them who wore suits very similar to his, and carried lasers. They couldn't breathe the thin, poisonous atmosphere either for they also had small tanks on their back as well.

When they discovered the ship was empty, they started to turn away. Jeff jumped, floating towards them, opened fire, and shot one in the back. The blast killing him instantly, as the other leaped towards the ship, only to be killed by an explosion Jeff had thrown, and destroyed part of their craft in the process.

The smoke cleared, and Jeff saw the inside of the black craft through the hole the explosive had made. He approached the ship, careful to make sure there weren't any other aliens to retaliate against him. The writing on the side appeared to be hieroglyphics, but it was not from Earth or displayed Earth-like origins. When Jeff entered, he noticed there was seating for two pilots only, even though the ship was a great deal larger than his own, approximately one hundred and fifty feet wide to be exact.

The control panel was similar to his, but he was unable to decipher the writing. He noticed a flashing red light on the panel was activated, but wasn't sure if it was a rescue beacon or a self destruct mechanism and didn't want to stick around to find out. He opened the compartment located next to the escape hatch, and took two extra laser guns and two small black spherical objects which he didn't know the use of. He jumped from the craft and approached the alien closest to his ship. Jeff pulled his helmet off, and stared in disbelief. The creature was simian in appearance, with one eye in the middle of its grotesque head which was covered with thick, black fur. He photographed the alien with a device about the size of a flash drive, and jumped back into his ship. He shut the main door lock, and replaced his power supply cartridge with the only one of his own left, and switched on the control panel.

The ship's sensors indicated that there were two crafts moving at a high velocity towards the surface. He fired the main thruster rockets and escaped as fast as he could, but not before being struck broadside by their photonic weapons. His control panel shorted out just after he escaped the atmosphere, leaving him weaponless, motionless, and floating through empty space. During this time, a piece of metal fell from the ceiling and knocked him unconscious.

When he finally awoke, he found that somehow he was spared. He laid on a beach of an uncharted planet billions of miles from Pluto he thought, unaware of how he got there or how to return home. Fortunately his ship was also spared, which he found miraculous in itself, but it was still in pretty rough shape. When he rose to his feet, he was greeted by the amphibian beings who called themselves lingworts.

It was now two and a half years from that day and an especially hot August afternoon on the tropical island, close to 105°. There weren't any clouds to shelter the heat, and Jeff sweated fiercely as he worked on repairing his ship. He kept a jug of fresh water next to him, in case he needed it. Dormiton, his closest friend among the tribe approached him from the far end of the beach.

"What are you doing?" he asked, scratching his smooth, slender head, as he entered the spaceship.

"Trying to repair my control panel," Jeff answered. "I don't know if I'll ever get this thing off the ground."

"Is it that bad?" Dormiton asked, not understanding even what a control panel was.

"If I don't repair it, I'll be stuck here forever. Besides, we need lasers in case aliens show up. I won't be able to fix the ship for space travel, however. I don't think I'll ever be able to repair the shields."

"Lasers?" he asked.

"Weapons."

"Oh. I doubt that you'll ever need them here, "Dormiton stated, as he sat in the extra pilot seat.

"Better safe than sorry," Jeff said as he wiped the sweat from his forehead.

"Why would anyone want to attack us, Jeff? It doesn't help to gather food or please the gods. Besides, we have nothing anyone would want other than the island itself."

"It may sound senseless to you, but you'd be surprised. They may want your people as a slave race. You have to fight to protect your people. There will come a day when you have enemies, and you must defeat them to survive. You can't depend on me forever."

"What enemies could we possibly have here?" the green, slender, spotted amphibian jested, and threw his thin arms in the air.

"Your own gods can be your enemies, "Jeff answered. "When I first came here, you thought I was a god. If I came from the stars, there could be others. They may not be as peaceful as I am, and you need to be prepared."

"Are you saying that our gods are really star people like you? You are speaking bad tongue, and could be killed for saying such!" His tone was serious, and reminded him of the ancient customs that they swore to uphold as a race.

"No, I'm not saying that at all. What I am saying, is that you shouldn't trust every god that falls from the sky. If I wasn't peaceful, I could have easily killed your small community. What you need is something to protect you, like gunpowder."

"What's gunpowder?"

"It's a type of powder that can be lit by a fire, but it goes out quickly. It

8

helps project an object, such as a rock, through a cylinder of some kind. My only regret is that if I show you how to use it, I might change your entire future."

"In what way?"

"I'd rather not discuss it now," Jeff said, as he finished soldering some wires shut the control panel faceplate, and smiled. "Besides that, Buddy, we have to see if this beast will run." Dormiton shut the main door lock and they put their helmets and safety belts on.

"Is Milgic meeting us at the village later?" Jeff asked, and switched on the main power supply and fired the ion propulsion rockets. Dormiton nodded instead of talking over the noise of the engine.

The craft rose slow above the white beach and Jeff switched on the main rockets, which elevated the craft over the ocean higher and faster. He reached an elevation of about eight thousand feet, when he suddenly noticed a light on his right side. It looked like a spaceship, but was too far away to determine if it was of the same nature as the ones he saw on Pluto.

When it came closer, he knew his intuition had been correct. The craft was similar to the one he had seen two years before, spherical in shape and black in color. Jeff navigated his ship closer, moved up to about mock eight, when the craft made a direct curve to his left. The Martian's ship imitated its movements exactly, as it plunged towards the ocean. Dormiton swallowed in fear, afraid they would meet a fiery, watery death.

"Relax," Jeff told his friend as he smiled. "It's only a test run." Jeff closed in on the craft and reached for his laser controls. Upon firing, the panel short-circuited again.

"Damn it," he hissed, and tried to retreat, only to be struck from behind. The ship spiraled out of control towards the sea below them. Smoke billowed from the tail section, and Jeff in haste reached for the ejection lever. Upon pulling it, the escape pod piloted the two safely from the craft, which now struck the ocean in a blazing inferno. Fortunately they landed in water near the shoreline.

It had been a rough landing, but neither one of them were hurt. They climbed from what was left of the ship and waded towards the shore. When they reached the beach, Jeff slammed his helmet in the sand in anger. "I'm never going home now," he snapped, peering out at the sinking wreckage of the ship.

"Can you build a new one?" his friend asked, unaware of the magnitude of the situation.

"It's not that simple," Jeff laughed. "I need materials and processes that don't exist here, such as metal and fabrication of the metal."

"What does it look like?"

"It's silver colored and shiny!" Jeff said, annoyed by his ignorance. "Just forget it! I'm stranded here and there's nothing anyone can do about it!"

"I've seen what you seek," Dormiton told him.

Jeff who was surprised, and quite interested, asked, "Where?"

"Behind that cove over there." He pointed to the ridge that overlooked the ocean at the opposite end of the beach, about three miles away. "Every morning when the sun rises, three lights fly from the water where this 'metal' you speak of is. They vanish into the sky, almost as if they're there and then gone."

"The lights have to be spaceships. An alien race could have a base here. We'll climb that ridge tomorrow to get a better look. In the meantime, we need to go back to the village and get everyone to a safe place, like the caves on the other side of the island. Tell them a storm is coming. We don't know what we're dealing with yet, and we don't want anyone to be alarmed."

Learning from past cultures helped Jeff to understand his new companions. From many civilizations in Earth's past, he learned to deal with more primitive people, assisting them in development, and protecting their vulnerability to their enemies: especially themselves. Earthlings almost made themselves extinct, along with other species of animals that were killed off. It took three global wars for man to realize there would never be a victor. The third war happened at a time when peace had almost been achieved. He hadn't only confined his studies to Earth or Mars however. Their probes traveled throughout their galaxy collecting information on intelligent life. He never actually met an alien face to face however; until that cold stormy day on Pluto.

Jeff showed the Lingwort community how to construct huts from straw, wood, and clay, and how to seal them so they would be waterproof. He had learned how to do this in the tropical biodome on Mars during his survival training in the academy. The village consisted of thirty lingworts, mostly males. The rest of their clan was supposed to arrive in three lunar cycles. They were migrating from a smaller island in search of food. Scouts had already been sent back when Jeff arrived at the island.

The sun set on the small village, which was at the edge of the jungle. The village was lit rather well that night because of their precautions to depart to the caverns. Dinner consisted of the usual vegetables, herbs, and fruit, except for a small goose that Jeff captured earlier and ate. Eating meat or killing animals was sacrilege to the Lingworts, but they made an exception for small insects and fish that they could swallow whole. Even though they didn't believe in this, they were tolerant of their new friend's cuisine. Game was plentiful on the island, and he didn't miss an opportunity.

After dinner, the townspeople gathered their gear and placed it on their backs. Dormiton and Jeff led them into the jungle, followed by their trustworthy friend, Milgic. Milgic was probably the most influential of all the villagers, and the most curious. He was slightly more outspoken than Dormiton and quite a bit more pessimistic, which led Jeff to wonder how they ever became such close friends.

Lingworts were like four feet salamanders to him, but no, a little bit of a frog too. He couldn't explain how they were able to talk, but somehow they did. Even before he taught them English, they had spoken in their own native tongue. Jeff knew they had vocal cords, and small blunt teeth, but couldn't explain how they

10

developed a language. Their race reminded him of ancient tribesmen on Earth. It was plain to see why they were gatherers and hadn't learned to kill yet. This presented its own share of problems when other wild animals attacked. They would mostly run to wherever they could find refuge. Jeff wanted to keep violence out of their lives, but he also knew it was a necessary evil sometimes. The troop dressed in thick clothing to avoid being bit by mosquitoes that were two inches long and deadly. In addition to Malaria, one also expected to get nasty skin infection that permanently scarred for life, considering you're still alive to begin with. They carried the serum with them at all times, made of some roots on the island. Jeff was not allowed to know what they were, it was sacred and used only by their "Hodiku," or "medicine chief." Jeff showed them how he made his own medicines from roots and herbs as well, something he had been taught in his early academy days. Jeff carried a dagger with him, as well as a laser gun in case they were attacked.

About three hours passed when they came to a clearing to rest. There was considerably less humidity in the air then there was the previous evening, but it was still a hot evening. Jeff handed Dormition a canteen, and gestured for him to pass it to Milgic, who dropped his pack to the ground.

Jeff suggested that they spend the night at the clearing because the caves were still over a mile away. He told them not to light any fires because they didn't know what they were facing yet. Jeff was nervous about the whole situation and couldn't sleep anyway, so he took the first watch while the others slept.

The night was uneventful and by the time they reached the caverns it was near noon. Jeff instructed them to wait at the entrance while he investigated a cavern with Dormiton. He lit a torch and handed to his comrade. The human went first, prepared to fire his laser if he needed to. They came to two tunnels that went in alternate directions. "Wait here," Jeff told him. "One of us should stay here in case we need to warn the others."

They entered the tunnel on the right, and Jeff noticed a concentrated white cool gas with no odor and nonpoisonous. The tunnel was made of metal that he wasn't familiar with, and it was well-lit. Someone constructed it, and he knew it couldn't have been the lingworts.

Jeff came upon two metal doors at the end. He must have accidentally tripped them, because they opened and revealed another hallway. Startled, he gripped his laser tight and was cautious to look in all directions. He decided it was clear, and entered the hallway on his right until he reached another door. He should have gone back and told the others, but his curiosity grew as he ventured further. The door didn't open at first, but after he pressed one of the four buttons on the side panel, it responded.

There was a flight of metal stairs, which led to a huge control center. He never saw such an array of computers in all of his years as an astronaut. There were men, or at least they looked like men running them. He couldn't tell because they were all wearing helmets.

Looking beyond the machinery, he saw several large spaceships, much like the ones he had seen on Pluto, and over the ocean. They were black and spherical, with fins on their sides. There were too many of the aliens wandering around for him to do any more exploring at the moment.

Jeff wondered why they wanted to build a base on their planet. Perhaps it was a scientific research station? An alien race could learn something from the geographical features and the climate. On the other hand, if it was a battle outpost, nothing could be gained by landing here; there was really nothing to conquer. The only possibility he could surmise was that they were hiding from an enemy force. Sooner or later, they would discover the village and no one knew if they were friend or foe. Jeff went back to where Dormiton was, careful not to be spotted. He grabbed the torch from the amphibian's hand and gestured for him to leave the cave.

"There's an alien complex down there," he told his friends. "How long it's been there, I don't know. I'll help you escape, but once I know you're all safe, I'm going to try to find a way to pilot one of their ships and leave this place. I've got to get back to Mars. I'll miss you guys, but it's really for the best. I need people."

"Why don't you just ask them if they'll trade something for one?" asked Milgic, unaware of the seriousness of the situation.

"Because I have no indication of whether this race is hostile or not," Jeff answered. They may kill all of us if they find us. No, the best thing is for all of you to get out of here until I find out what this is all about."

"Where will we go?" asked one of the Lingworts.

"We'll need to build rafts and get you off this island," Jeff told them. "You'll be safe that way."

"And what will you do?" Dormiton asked, quite worried.

"You can't just leave us," Milgic snapped.

"What do you expect from me?" Jeff asked. "I've shown how to build, grow your own food, and fight if you need to. The time has come to return to my own kind. Your people have to defend yourselves. What would happen if I died? You'd have to fight. I've shown you how to make spears, bows, and arrows, but it's up to you to use them."

Lingwort was very grateful to Jeff, and it seemed hideous to leave them vulnerable to attack knowing that moving to another island was only a temporary solution. However, he had needs of his own to attend to. He was homesick, and didn't want to spend the rest of his life with aliens. This may have been his only opportunity to escape this world and get back to his own kind, wherever that may be. He didn't believe he was being unreasonable.

"We want to go with you," cried Dormiton. Jeff could tell how much Dormiton loved him and respected him.

"Absolutely not!" he retorted. "You couldn't survive in space with me. It's full of unknown dangers and hostile environments. I have no guarantee that I'll even reach my destination. Do you really believe a being of peace, such as you, can survive in an environment of war?"

"I'm no longer afraid to take risks," Dormtion stated. "I won't let you leave by yourself! It's too dangerous, and you need someone to help you!"

Dormtion was right about that. Jeff couldn't very well charge into the complex and steal a spaceship without being seen. An operation of this nature needed planning and at least two people, if not a whole army. He saw no other alternative than to agree with him.

"Very well, "he said. "I'll take two, and only two of you with me. However, the minute I hear any complaints I'm gonna throw you in the ejection capsule and send you to the nearest planet. The rest of you can get off this island somehow; perhaps we can build a raft and launch it from the back cove. Once you're off the island, you'll be safe. Right now we have to find shelter, so follow me."

Jeff was just leading his troop back into the jungle, when he heard a noise from the rocks above. Someone fired a weapon, and Jeff's weapon flew from his hand. He grabbed his hand, stinging in pain.

"Don't move!" a voice called from above. Jeff turned, confronting an army of the same beings he saw on Pluto. He wondered what type of gas they were breathing. He knew it wasn't oxygen because they wore spacesuits and tanks on their backs. The leader gestured for two of the men to grab Jeff. They each grabbed one of his arms and yanked them behind his back.

"Who are you?" he asked, as he walked down from the hill. The lingworts were frozen in a state of shock at these militant beings, too scared to fight or flee. They always thought Jeff was invincible and god-like, and to see him in a compromising position was shocking to them. The leader walked over to him and examined him thoroughly.

"I asked you a question, human," he sneered. "A spy for the Galactic Republic no doubt." Jeff wasn't overjoyed about the fact that he suspected him of being a spy, but had no choice but to listen to what he said. When he didn't answer, the creature struck him across the jaw. Jeff was weakened from struggling to get loose because the aliens were stronger than he was. He wasn't sure he could take one of them, let alone three.

"You'll talk sooner or later, when your friends die off one by one," he threatened.

"Wait!" Jeff pleaded. "I'm not a spy; I'm an astronaut for the Martian space academy! I've been stranded on this island for two years! I don't even know how I got here!"

"Lies" the leader screeched. He raised his laser towards Jeff's friends. Jeff struggled as he fired, and two of the Lingworts vanished instantly in a flash of light, leaving only smoke where they had stood. The others watched in disbelief and fear. "Maybe now you'll talk?"

"All right," Jeff pleaded. "I'll tell you whatever you want to know, just don't kill any-more of my friends!" He approached the human, and pointed the gun in

13

his face.

"What do you know? Perhaps you are a Republic spy? What can you tell me of Mars, Human? You cannot survive on such a planet without oxygen. You are lying. Why are you here? What brings a human this far out?" He knew that Jeff was telling the truth. It was obvious to Jeff he was playing a malicious game of some kind.

"I was marooned on this planet for two years," Jeff explained. "I have no ship because your men destroyed it. I live with these beings, and we are peaceful. We are no threat to you."

"If you are not Tolarion, you are a threat to us," he grunted and shoved the gun in the human's mouth.

"We just want to live in peace!" Jeff insisted one last time, the coldness of the steel weapon against his lips.

"Peace is for the weak," the cyclopic alien laughed. "Take them to the complex for extermination; all except Major Walker. I want to have a talk with him." Walker wasn't surprised the leader knew his name due to the incident on Pluto, and he would probably be executed along with his friends. Jeff watched, as the lingworts were pushed into the tunnel like a herd of cattle.

Tears ran from Dormiton's cheeks as he stared at his companions in fear. They didn't understand what was about to happen to them, or understand why the newcomers behaved in such a manner.

Jeff was unable to determine what his captors had in store for him, or where he was being taken. They directed him down a passageway with four doors, until they came upon the last door. He didn't see any writing on the doors, which made it difficult for him to know where he was going when he needed to escape. They entered the doorway, which opened on its own into a laboratory. He scanned the room, which contained equipment that was unfamiliar to him. The containers they used to hold specimens were flat and circular. There weren't any test tubes visible; only round, glass balls. The leader spoke in a foreign tongue to his followers, gesturing for them to leave the room. He still kept his laser pointed at Jeff, removing his helmet. He was wearing some kind of mask over his nostrils and mouth, but Jeff could still hear his voice.

"Sit down," he said, pushing him into the chair. "I'll spare your friends-if you tell me the location of the Sentronian base and your own planet."

"You've already found my planet," Jeff responded, as his mind raced for an avenue of escape. The odds were more even now, and he was sure he could overcome their leader.

"You are lying! You are not from here, you are from Mars! I need to know where the Martians have hidden their race."

"Why?"

"That's for me to know," he laughed and bared a wicked grin, which Jeff saw through his transparent respirator. "Forgive me, Mr. Walker. I have been rude to my guest. I haven't introduced myself properly. Balta is my name, imperial leader of the Tolarion Army. I already know who you are. You are Major Jeff Walker, of the Martian colony. You shouldn't be surprised that I know you. After all, it was you who killed two of my best agents and pilfered their ship. To me, it's small offense, but still unforgiveable. Well, your people are no longer on your puny red planet. They have left, and I want to know where they have gone!"

"Why punish others for what I have done?"

"Because it is insurance that you will tell me what I need to know. If you don't, your friends will die."

"Why should your kind rule the galaxy?" Jeff asked, as he reached for one of the glass balls behind him.

"Keep your hands where I can see them!" Balta barked, and pointed the gun at Jeff's chest "I won't tolerate anymore defiance!"

"I don't suppose you will," the Martian said, as he struggled to take the laser from Balta's hand. With his free hand Jeff grabbed a glass ball which contained acid, and smashed it on the alien's hand. He fell to the floor and clutched his hand in severe pain. Jeff grabbed his laser and struck him over the head, which rendered him unconscious. Jeff fired the laser at the door, blasting a huge hole in it, providing his means of escape. The two guards were on the floor, and Jeff ran down the corridor until he came upon a large red door. It was partially open, revealing four guards in front of a brig of some kind. Dormiton and Milgic were the only prisoners in it, both of them frightened and crying.

He knew he was outnumbered, so he had to think of a good plan. He thought about the direct approach, but also thought that all of Balta's men would come down, and abandoned that idea. There wouldn't be much of an escape if the alarm was sounded. Jeff quietly backed up in the corridor, took a stone he picked up from the cavern floor earlier and threw it in the opposite direction than where he was. Two of the guards heard the sound and headed down the corridor, and Jeff came up from behind and smashed their helmets together which dazed them, and they fell to the floor. The other guards heard the commotion and opened fire. Jeff fired back at them, rolled his body across the floor, just missing a blast. He fired back, hit one of them in the head and shattered his skull like a crushed pineapple. The other one escaped and set the alarm off. He fought them off for the moment, but more would be on the way. When he reached the brig, he immediately destroyed the force field controls with his laser, and released his friends.

"Jeff!" Dormition yelled in relief. "You're all right!" He grabbed him around the waist in comfort."

"We have to get out of here," Jeff stated, as he grabbed his arm. Milgic quickly followed.

"Grab their guns!" Jeff commanded. The lingworts stared at him, unwilling to comply. Neither one would touch them. "Never mind, let's just get out of here!"

They heard the loud ringing throughout the complex, as the trio headed down the corridor, unaware of where they were headed. Jeff kept his laser ready, as the sound of footsteps could be heard behind them, getting closer and closer. They ran faster until they came to two very large doors, and Jeff pressed the button that opened them. He had to buy some time, so he ran to the nearest door panel and pressed the main door lock. It would take them a while to cut through the thick metal, working to his advantage.

The controls were written in English, which didn't make much sense to him. Why would a race so far away from Earth or Mars, write English and speak English as well as their own native tongue? Maybe they had been watching humans for some time. They piloted spacecraft much faster than anything humans developed, and their computers were far more advanced than any he ever saw, but weren't impossible to decipher, for Jeff had extensive knowledge of computer systems. The ringing sound of the alarm made his hands a little jumpy, but after a few minutes, he felt a little calmer. He tried to tap into the mainframe, but was unsuccessful, and he didn't have much time to play around, so he abandoned his efforts and moved away from the machine.

"Stand back!" he told his friends, and aimed his laser at the computer. He fired, and it exploded and smoked. He pointed to an air duct and blasted the grating with his laser. He gestured for them to get in the air duct, bent down, and allowed them to climb on his shoulders. Jeff threw his gun up to them as the sound of the guards cutting through the door intensified. They worked themselves down the duct until they were well out of distance. They would be safe until they reached the end, where there was sure to be a welcoming committee.

Jeff's grandfather once told him that fear could either help someone or hurt someone, depending on what the situation was. He claimed that when a man was cornered, he was no different than a wild animal, and fear could be used as a dangerous weapon. Death was not something to be afraid of, and it was just a final phase in the cycle of life; a bridge to the hereafter.

Jeff always dreamed what it would be like without war, disease, or famine. Living in Lingwort was just about as close to this dream he would ever get. Even this peaceful world seemed to become a battleground when the mood was set. Jeff himself didn't realize it at the time, but he had already poisoned their little peaceful community. He already shown them the first step of what it means to be human-he taught them how to kill.

16

CHAPTER TWO

It was early evening by the time they reached the end of the air duct. There was a metal grating at the end that overlooked a heavily guarded spaceship hangar deck. They were near enough to the floor for Jeff to jump down, and at the moment no one was looking. The spaceships were not far from him, perhaps three hundred feet at the most. There were at least twenty aliens near them, and another thirty were moving freely about the deck. To steal a ship, he needed a plan, and quick.

He drew a deep breath, and sat there thinking for what seemed an eternity. The sweat was pouring from his forehead from the heat of the vent behind him. There were too many of them for him to charge them, so that approach was out of the question. He eyed the room carefully, but saw no way out. The only possible alternative he saw was a small, black tank on the far side of the deck, which contained some kind of concentrated gas. He turned to his friends with an idea which would be crude, but effective.

"Guys," he whispered to them. "After I remove this metal grating, I want you to stay here until I shoot at that black oval object over there. After I do, I want you to run as fast as you can to the first ship on the right. I'll be right behind you." They backed up, while Jeff got ready to kick the grating. After he kicked the grating off, he jumped down and fired his laser at the tank. The tank exploded before the aliens could fire back at him, sending a plume of flames and smoke through the deck, and killing at least half of them. The explosion knocked Jeff to the floor and Milgic and Dormiton out of the vent. They rose to their feet, dazed.

"Run to the ships!" Jeff yelled, as an alien grabbed his arm. He punched him with his right hand in his stomach. He fell, and Jeff reached for his laser. Another guard ran towards him, only to be obliterated by the blast of the laser gun. Milgic was shot in the leg by one of the aggressors and screamed in agony, as his amphibian friend dragged him in haste into the spaceship. Jeff followed closely behind, and there was a barrage of laser fire. The hangar deck was in flames, and half of guards tried to extinguish it.

The other half tried to stop Jeff as he ran towards the craft and jumped in, pressing the hatch door button. The inside of the craft was considerably different than his. It was hemi- spherical shape, and had many more controls. The one thing that surprised him was that everything in it was written in English as well as hieroglyphics. Jeff didn't see any problems learning how to pilot it. The majority of the ship was set up like his own, with a helm and weapons system. There was seating for three, and a main screen area. It covered with computers, except for the rear, where the sleeping quarters and storage was. The interior was rather large, at least one hundred and ten feet in diameter. There was also a surgical area, with a table in the middle of it, where Dormiton placed his friend. As he sat at the helm, he heard their pursuers cutting through the door with their lasers. Jeff himself started to get nervous as he tried to figure out how to switch on the engines.

"Get him strapped in!" Jeff yelled to Dormiton, who began to panic.

"They're getting in!" He yelled.

"Get him strapped in!" Jeff yelled again. It reminded him of the incident on Pluto two years earlier. He was pretty sure now that the Tolarions were responsible for the invasion, if there was one, of the Mars base. The evidence was overwhelming.

He fired the lifter rockets, and Dormiton responded to his command, and strapped his friend to the surgical table located about thirteen feet from the helm on the left side of the ship. He strapped himself in and fired the thruster rockets as Dormiton joined him at the helm. The blast was quite powerful and the landing deck wasn't designed to withstand the full force of them. Jeff was unsure of what type of propulsion they used, but he guessed it was at least fusion powered. The building collapsed around them and they entered a long metal tunnel that seemed endless. Jeff determined that it was constructed to pilot spacecraft down it to pick up speed the further they went through. It seemed to be straight, until they came to a slight inclination at the end. When the craft emerged from the tunnel, they were overlooking the cove and the island of Lingwort. The metal object that Dormiton had seen a few days before was nothing more than an underwater launch pad for ships.

Jeff felt sad he couldn't save all of his friends. He knew the remaining lingworts were at the mercy of the Tolarions and there was no hope for them. There was no way he could fight their whole military, but he reasoned he could attack them at the source. It meant, however, that he would also have to kill any other prisoners as well. It was not an easy decision to make, but he knew it was for the good of this planet. He checked the scanners for enemy craft, and then circled the mountain range twice. He prepared to attack what was left of the base, as he struggled with feelings of fear, guilt, and anger. When he fired the photonic lasers, the ridge was engulfed by the explosion. There was no counter-attack, and after the smoke cleared, there wasn't any base either. The ridge crumbled into a massive pile of rocks, with no visible life.

They traveled farther into the atmosphere, and Dormiton was marveled by the beauty of this insignificant ball that he lived upon and called "masrigia," or home. He began to realize how small his little island was and the enormous size of the universe. They both took a moment to reflect on their loss, and the memories they permanently left behind. Their home was destroyed, and their place where they shared happiness, tranquility, joy, and fulfillment was lost.

Jeff ascended the craft towards space, and thought about how both races could have been spared. The whole battle could have been avoided if the Tolarions had just given the time to move back to their own island. That seemed unlikely, however, because they were up against a dictator who wanted to use their tiny little island for the wrong purposes.

What of Lingwort, a race that didn't have the intelligence or technology to even defend themselves against their invaders? They were accused of crimes they didn't commit, and if there were any survivors, they wouldn't trust beings from the skies ever again. Their idealistic society was no longer peaceful. Jeff was saddened by this because he had grown accustomed to the quiet and solitude, and also knew they were about to face dangerous and unknown challenges.

Jeff noticed the ship moved much faster than his wreck, and within a short time, the small five planet system in which Lingwort was a part of was far behind them. As they passed through the orb cloud barrier that surrounded this system, the ship shook a little and passed through with a minimal amount of effort, and the darkness of space closed in on them. He told Dormiton to hang on while he advanced the ship to interstellar speed. In ten minutes, they were billions of miles from where they had been. He guessed that it involved either electromagnetic forces of some kind, fusion, or even antimatter propulsion to travel such a great distance in a short period of time. He couldn't understand how the ship was shielded from meteors, comets, and radiation, but he guessed it was some kind of special process that Martians couldn't comprehend. After he considered himself to be at a safe distance, he switched controls to auto-pilot, and the two of them went back to help their friend Milgic. Jeff looked at Milgic's wound carefully.

"How is he?" asked Dormiton. Jeff examined him to see if his eyes were dilated or had a pulse.

"He's got a bad burn on his left leg," Jeff stated. "He'll be in shock for a little while, but I think he'll make it. Put some bandages tightly around his wound. We have to find something to cover him with." Dormiton reached inside a nearby compartment, pulling out a spacesuit. He handed it to the human, and he placed it over his friend. "You better put a suit on also. Find a short one, if you can."

"He always was strong-willed," Dormiton said, as Jeff searched for some pain medicine. He found bandages to wrap the wound, and handed them to his friend. Dormiton struggled to put the spacesuit on. They had no tails, but it was rather large for him.

"Now do you believe all gods are not peaceful?" Jeff lectured, as he zipped up his friend's suit.

"You were right, Jeff. I should have listened to you. My people were all killed by them, and we did nothing to stop them. Why did they want to kill us? We would have shared the island with them?" He felt now that he had been too trusting of the Tolarions.

"This race is not interested in sharing. They have no respect for other races, only ideas of conquest and enslavement."

"Why would anybody want that?"

"Power, my friend, power. My grandparents' home planet had the same problem. That's why it destroyed itself. We're dealing with a very hostile race that is bent on destruction."

"What do you mean we're dealing with them? Didn't you destroy their base?"

"That was only the beginning. There are probably many more of them somewhere else, and they're going to be very angry when they find out what's happened."

"Didn't you say that you're people eventually became peaceful? Can't we somehow find peace with these beings?"

"Yes, it's possible, but only if this race wants peace and that is doubtful. They are a very violent race."

Dormiton wrapped the bandages tightly around Milgic's wound and then taped it with surgical tape. While his companion watched over his friend, Jeff walked over to the helm and checked a panel which contained the life support system controls. Much to his surprise there were only two controls; one for oxygen distribution and the other for nitrogen distribution. There were also levels for each, which meant in his mind that these Tolarions not only breathed nitrogen, but also oxygen, unless it was used for another purpose. It was currently switched to oxygen, and the level was at 18%, which surprised him because it was the same concentration as Earth's.

"We've got enough oxygen to keep us going until we know where we are," Jeff said. "I don't know what our friends, the Tolarions, eat, but whatever it is, it'll have to do. There must be a star charting system in the computer system to tell us where we're going."

Jeff stared at the assortment of computers, and knew it would be difficult to decipher some of their codes. Even if he was able to bring up the charting system, it would be impossible to understand it fully. The stars and planets probably had different names and locations that he was unfamiliar with. He turned on a small visual scanner that revealed a star chart; a lucky guess on his part. Sure enough, the stars were unfamiliar to him.

"Oh Boy," he said. "I think we're lost."

"What are we going to do now," Dormiton asked.

Jeff really had no plan of what to do next. "I don't know," he stated. "I guess we're going to have to find a planet where there's an oxygen based atmosphere. We'll have to stay there as long as we can. They'll be looking for us, and when they find us, they'll kill us. If they want us, they'll have to catch us first. If I can somehow figure out how to alter the engines, which is a big if, I might be able to get a little more speed out them. It'll be risky, though."

"How risky?"

"Risky enough to blow us up into a million pieces!"

"I was afraid you'd say something like that."

Jeff surmised the computers on the ship were highly advanced, much more than his race was. He knew they were controlling a propulsion system of some kind, but what kind? Ion and fusion based systems seemed to slow to be able to travel such great distances. It had to be electromagnetism or anti-matter, or perhaps even Planck technology, he just wasn't sure. As he read across the various panels, he came across two buttons marked "dimensional transporter" and "dimensional tracker." He consulted the main computer for a definition of the controls.

"Computer operative," a male voice said. Jeff was surprised because his race didn't' yet discover how to create a voice-activated system that could run an entire starship. "Dimensional transporter is used by the Tolarion government to enable a spacecraft to be undetected by alien craft by transporting the vessel into another universe or the same universe at a different location by using antimatter and dark energy and the density of a nearby star or black hole as a catalyst to generate a wormhole," the computer stated. He heard of the theory of parallel universes and wormhole travel but they were just theories and no one ever produced solid proof of their existence. It amazed him a race could even come up with such technology. He turned to Dormiton to tell him what he discovered.

"That explains it," he said. "Why you saw lights in the sky, and why they vanished. It seems that this ship possesses a device that enables it to travel to another place, and return from that place. That's why they appeared invisible."

"You mean it's there, but you can't see it?" surmised Dormiton.

"Something like that," Jeff said to simplify. "The enemy will probably be looking for us after they've found out I've destroyed their base. I'm pretty sure that your planet is not their home planet. We can also track them, too. If one decides to tail us, we could destroy him first."

"How?"

"They're not going to fire first for one reason. Unless they've found out about the base, as far as they know, we are one of them. All we have to do is send a distress signal to them, and when they prepare to dock with us, we blow them away."

"Just like that, huh?" His amphibian friend was a bit more skeptical. "Besides, then we'll be in real trouble by their government. Haven't enough died already? Why do you have to make matters worse?"

Jeff was getting a little disgusted with his pacifist attitude. "They kill your people for no reason, they accuse them of being spies, and you want me to do nothing? I'm just giving them a little justice in return. Now, you may disagree with my ethics, but sooner or later you'll realize that there is no peace worth keeping if your freedom is taken away!"

Dormiton remained silent for hours after that, as he watched close over his friend. What Jeff didn't understand is why he felt no anger towards their attackers. He was becoming more defensive, but it would still be a while before he was willing to fight. Their alien counterparts were much the opposite with their militant characteristics. Either side asked the impossible. It wouldn't only be a mistake on their part to befriend the Tolarions, but it would have been an open invitation for them to destroy what was left of the Lingwort race. Jeff couldn't let them do that.

They ventured nine hundred billion miles since their week departure; an idea which neither of them could easily grasp. The Martian space academy had nothing that could compare with the velocity of this craft, and he was extremely impressed with its agility.

They came upon a planet, and Jeff switched the engines to sub-orbital speed. While he gazed at the helm panel, he came across a button marked investigative probe." When he pressed it, the ship released a small probe that fired like a missile toward the planet. Digesting the computer's data, he learned the probe analyzed gases and atmospheric conditions. It was similar to Martian or old Earth probes, but much more advanced. He watched it until it vanished from sight onto the surface of the bluish-green world.

Not more than thirty seconds had passed, and he was already receiving a multitude of information. The probe indicated that the world was 2,000,000 miles from the ship, 350,000,000 miles from its sun, and 20,000 miles in diameter. The atmosphere consisted of nitrogen, methane, carbon, and helium. The surface was mostly ice and barren rock, consisting of both active and inactive geyser activity with temperatures ranging from –250 degrees to –500 degrees. In short, it was a very cold and barren place incapable of sustaining any life as they knew it.

Before he had given up total hope, he reminded himself of the dimensional transporter. He wondered if it would be possible to scan for a planet in another dimension without traveling there. He consulted the computer for an answer.

"Computer," he said.

"Operative," it replied.

"Is it possible to scan for life forms in another dimension?"

"Negative."

Discouraged, he tapped his finger on the control panel, raised his dark brown eyebrow and contemplated whether to press the transporter controls. He didn't know what result it would produce or what it would do to them physically. However, their air was going to run out and they needed refuge somewhere. He pressed the button and felt a tremendous pull on the craft from the engine, as the nearest star began to get brighter, and sent a flare millions of miles into space from it, and a beam of light emerged from the front of the ship and intersected the flare, producing a wormhole. Jeff stared ahead in disbelief, as he watched particles of a black substance emerge from the ship into the beam and towards the wormhole.

"What now," he asked.

"Do you think we should go through it?" Dormiton asked.

"I really don't think we have a choice." He pressed the velocity button, took a deep breath and the ship propelled forward, entering the wormhole. When it did, they became extremely dizzy for ten seconds and almost blacked out, as the ship spiraled through the tunnel of space and time. When they regained their senses, they were staring in amazement at the huge green planet in front of them. Dormiton stumbled to the helm, and the wormhole closed up instantaneously and disappeared into empty space.

"Did you see that?" he asked. Jeff nodded, bewildered. He gathered now there were at least three universes, not just one. He launched another probe, as Dormiton sat down beside his human companion. "How is he?"

"He's much better," Dormiton answered. "He's out of shock, and the burn wasn't too bad. They watched as the probe hit the world below them, which was two thirds water. The landmasses were not very large, and there were a few mountain ranges.

"He took a pretty hard hit," Jeff said.

"Yes, but our skin heals much faster than yours. We used to believe it was gift from the gods, until you showed us what medicine was."

Jeff began to realize that there was still much he didn't know about their race. Sure, he lived with them for two years, but he never saw anyone seriously hurt in that time. Dormiton seldom spoke about their culture, and some rituals, customs, and beliefs were forbidden to outsiders.

His thoughts were distracted by the transmissions the probe was sending him. The new planet, which the computer named Sirkis, was 25,000 miles from the ship, and located about 103,000,000 miles from its sun. The diameter of the 'super Earth' was 38,000 miles, and the surface temperatures ranged from 30 degrees to 65 degrees at the equator. The atmosphere contained a large presence of oxygen and nitrogen, as well as other elements. He decided to conduct further investigation, so he transmitted data to the probe. Within seconds, he received results. It stated that there were life forms on the surface, but it was mostly vegetation. There was some animal life, but extremely primitive.

Their oxygen was low, and if they had to land somewhere, this was as good a place as any. He cut the rockets to orbital speed, as they closed in on the planet. He turned on the heat shielding device, which he guessed was some more advanced form of polyethylene or derivative thereof, and prepared to enter the atmosphere. He directed Dormiton to look into a device used to indicate the angle of re-entry.

"What does it say?" he asked.

"Thirty five."

"Let's try to get it to about thirty eight degrees." Dormiton pressed the button that allowed the computer to make the necessary adjustments.

The one thing that amazed Jeff the most about Dormiton was his ability to learn. The only reason his culture hadn't advanced further was because of their stubbornness to hang on to their old systems and beliefs. Their customs needed to be preserved, but in their present situation, he also needed to learn the current technology they were using as well.

They descended towards the blue and white surface of the world. The ship floated in the atmosphere while Jeff checked his scanners. All of the sudden four objects appeared on the viewing screen. It was apparent he underestimated his pursuers. "Wait a minute," he said. "We got company!"

"The aliens?" Dormiton asked.

"You guessed it. The ships are identical to this one. They obviously have a base nearby. It didn't take them too long to find us. Well, so much for plan A. They know who we are."

"What's plan B?"

"We'll have to either outrun them or fight them head-on." Dormiton looked at him like he was insane, shook his head and said nothing.

He maneuvered the ship towards his attackers, and prepared to fire the main lasers. They were about three hundred thousand miles and closing. He was just about to fire, when another wormhole opened, and they disappeared into it.

"Enemy craft no longer in range," the computer stated. "Convert to dimensional tracker." Jeff was surprised that they transported through a wormhole. He thought for sure that they would just attack him.

Dormiton grabbed his arm and pointed to the screen, as a photonic laser beam moved towards the ship rapidly. They were still out there, all right, but out of range of his scanners. They were obviously much better at this game than he was.

"Defense shields on!" he yelled to the computer, just before they were struck. He pulled the vessel out, and was only hit mildly on the tail of the craft. "That was close!"

Dormiton sighed in relief that they were not blown to bits.

"What now," the amphibian asked his companion, as Jeff brought the engines to full power and the ship away from Sirkis.

"First thing is to get the hell out of here. We won't be landing on Sirkis. There's no guarantee they don't have a base down there. We can't even see what we're fighting against. You better look after Milgic. I'm gonna try to figure out what to do about our Tolarion friends."

He nodded, as he walked back to the surgical table. Milgic just awoke and tried to sit up, despite the straps holding him down. "You have to rest, my friend," he told him.

"Did we get away safely?" the weak Milgic asked.

"Yes." They made it safe off their world, but their world as they knew it changed in a way that would transform their future. Everyone they knew was either dead or on the other island. It saddened them to know they could never return there.

Jeff knew the computer wouldn't tell him where the ships went, so he relied on his own judgment. As he peered at the scanner, he could see they were tailed again. "How do you like that," he sneered, as Dormiton ran to the helm. "They're back! Well this time we'll just have to slow down and let them chase us. We might be able to get a couple of them with our rear lasers." The aliens closed in on him, he switched his rockets to sub-interstellar speed. He fired the photonic lasers and destroyed three of the four enemy craft in a beam of light and explosions. The fourth, however, moved much quicker and required more accuracy. Jeff switched on the interstellar drive to follow him.

"You'll never catch him," his amphibian friend challenged. The alien ship darted in front of him, and moved out of range. "Why don't you just let him go?"

"And have him report back to his superiors? Not a chance!" He followed the vessel as he closed in, it moved at a sharp angle, and then off the viewing screen. He had no idea where it had gone. "Damn! I almost had him! I've got to get better at this if I want to keep us alive!"

"What's that?" Dormiton asked, as he pointed to a flashing red light on the helm.

"The life support system failure light! We're losing oxygen!"

He sent out another probe, in hopes there was a planet nearby. It indicated there was a world called Belor with an atmosphere similar to Mars. It was mostly carbon dioxide, but there were traces of oxygen and nitrogen at the surface, in an enclosed structure of some kind. Gaseous clouds covered most of the planet, and acid rains ripped away at the already barren terrain.

Sensors also indicated there was arthropod life in a centralized colony within the structure that contained the nitrogen and oxygen. He was curious to see why insect life would be living there and nothing else. They must have breathed air, and were obviously not natives of this world, and must have some intelligence in order to build structures. It wasn't long before he received radio contact from the tiny reddish-green world. Much to his surprise, the transmission again was in English.

"This is Belor base," the voice said. "Alien craft, identify yourself." He was intrigued with the intelligence of this 'insect life.'

"This is Major Jeff Walker, of Mars, from the Milky way galaxy," Jeff answered. He eyed the ship to see if it had a name. He located it above the viewing screen. I'm a human flying an alien ship named the Rigil Four. I request to land on your base. We are out of oxygen and being chased by a Tolarion craft."

"What are you doing in a Tolarion craft?"

"We had to steal it to escape from them." There was a moment of silence.

"Very well. You will be permitted to land. We will be waiting."

Jeff didn't know if that was good or bad. What kind of creatures were they, and were they friendly or not? He turned on the heat shields and the sub-orbital rockets, and began to enter the atmosphere. It was almost impossible to see the surface through the reddish-colored clouds. It slowly became visible the closer they came. They felt a little breathless as the air started to give out. Jeff was prepared to get them to the jettison escape pod if necessary.

When they finally saw the surface, it was mostly rock. It was similar to the moon, with craters and dust over all of it. He guided the Rigil Four down to what appeared to him to be a runway. There were five domes that were all connected in the middle, and each dome had a red flashing light on top which were landing beacons. When they landed, they came upon two heavy metal doors that opened and revealed a hangar deck for spaceships. He docked rather rough, still a little not used to its functions, shut the engines down, and waited for their hosts. After a few minutes of quiet, Dormiton went back to help his friend. Before he could help him from off the table, the main door slid open and the aliens revealed themselves.

They didn't try to defy their orders because they knew they were trapped. The Tolarions would attack them if they left the atmosphere and if these Belorions were just as dangerous, then they didn't stand a chance here either. Besides, at the moment, they were the only allies they had.

He'd swear that they were a cross between an ant and a lobster. They were at least six to seven foot tall, had massive claws on all of their four arms, two large mandibles and were reddish in color. The human never saw an insect more advanced. They carried no weapons and wore headbands that glowed bright red, indicating that they might be used for that purpose. A large member of the group stepped forward.

"I am Zarcon," he announced, using thought messages that both the amphibians and Jeff could hear in their minds in their own languages. "The reason you heard our radio transmissions is because our minds can be used to transmit these frequencies." This should have alarmed Jeff, but he expected this much from a race as advanced as theirs. "And who might you be, Human?"

Jeff moved forward, but two of the aliens pulled him back. Apparently, they assumed he came in hostility. He relaxed his muscles, as he stared into the insect's dark, blue, compound eyes. "My name is Jeff Walker," he answered. "These are my friends Milgic and Dormiton. I came from a planet much like this one called Mars, which wouldn't be of any of your charts because it's in another universe, a parallel universe. We came here using what is called a dimensional transporter. The Tolarions attacked my friends' planet and we escaped in one of their ships. As far as I can tell, there are at least three universes that I know about."

Two of the Belorions, who were the other leaders, glanced at one another; then back at Jeff. "There are an infinite number of universes, Mr. Walker. This is the danger that the Tolarions have brought us," Zarcon said. Such a powerful tool is too advanced for such a hostile race. They could destroy everything that ever was created."

"How?" Jeff asked.

"They could change the multi-verse as we know it by altering a chain of events. Or they could disrupt the space-time continuum causing a rip in the universe similar to a warp of space and time. Where was the planet you were on when you were attacked?"

"I don't know. Before I arrived on my friends' planet, I lost control of my ship. My controls went haywire and I was left stranded in space. The last thing I remember is that I was by the dwarf planet Pluto. That was in the other universe-my universe."

"We will accept that as a satisfactory explanation of why you are here," he said, as he gestured for the guards to release him. "You will remain here until a further investigation can be conducted, if you don't mind. We'll try to make you as comfortable as possible. We'd also like to examine the Tolarion vessel as well."

"Certainly. What's on board that's so valuable? And how the hell do the Tolarions know about wormhole technology anyway? "

"We're just being cautious. We've made security mistakes in the past, and spies have come here. We'd like your cooperation. We don't suspect you are spies, but nonetheless, you'll have to answer some questions. We want to make sure also that you didn't bring any diseases with you. Is there any thing you need before I show you our little community?"

"No. Do you mind if I observe your inspection of our ship? There are a lot of devices I'm not familiar with, and I've got some catching up to do."

"As you wish. We know everything there is to know about the Tolarion Empire. Bolar, Kira, show these beings to the medical unit. One of them has a laser burn that needs attention." The insects nodded, and gently carried Milgic down the main corridor on a stretcher made from some form of white material similar to silk, only stronger.

"What type of propulsion system do these Tolarion ships use?" Jeff asked the large arthropod. "And how do they know how to travel through wormholes?"

"Antimatter," Zarcon answered. "The same technology that the Republic uses. You wouldn't understand the process, however. Not to be insulting, but it's way beyond your comprehension of Quantum physics. It involves the warping of space. Even your father of physics, Albert Einstein, wouldn't understand it. Even though they possess the ability, they didn't invent it. The Republic used it far longer, but more sparingly. It is likely that the Tolarions stole the process from us. They are foolishly playing with something that they only think they understand."

"That's the second time I've heard about this Republic. What is it, and who is this Balta character?"

"He is the leader of the Tolarions," Zarcon explained. "Why- have you met him?"

"You might say that," Jeff answered. "I killed him."

The large insect laughed in disbelief. "You killed him?"

"Yes, in the explosion of their base."

"Well," the insect stated. "If you did not see him actually die, he is probably not dead. He can be very resourceful when he wants to be."

"I see," the human answered, disappointed he didn't succeed. "What about this Republic?"

"They are the Galactic Republic of Peaceful Civilizations. I am the ambassador and ruler of this world, Belor. We work throughout our galaxy to maintain and endorse peace. Even humans like yourself are part of our alliance.

27

In fact, the council is located on a planet very similar to your ancestors'."

"And they obviously are against these Tolarions?"

"That is correct."

"How can I trust what you're telling me is the truth?" Zarcon then turned towards Jeff, his blue eyes fixed upon him.

"You may not trust me because I am frightening and strange to you," he jested. "I will show you that I mean you no harm. Mr. Walker, would you care to have a tour before retiring to your quarters?"

"I'd like that," Jeff said, as he smiled.

Jeff followed the Belorion, relaxed, but not fully convinced. Did he somehow get his friends and himself into a space war of some kind? What exactly were the motives of these giant insects, and how were they able to read minds? They claimed to be peaceful, but how could he know for sure? They were much more accommodating than the Tolarions, and didn't seem to have any hidden agendas. First impressions, however, sometimes could be deceiving.

CHAPTER THREE

Jeff followed Zarcon to the end of a long, oval shaped tunnel. Two doors opened and revealed a large room of computers. There were even more here than the Tolarion base on the island.

"This is our main control center," Zarcon replied. "With our advanced technology, we can find out anything we want to know within our galaxy. Is there anything that you wish to ascertain?"

"Where is Mars base, and how do I get there?"

"Computer operative," a voice answered. "Mars-the fourth planet around Sol, in the Milky Way galaxy, star sector 555-78-90, in alternate universe 34677."

"How long will it take to get there from here, even if I was to go back to my own universe using this vessel?"

"Three hundred and fifty nine years, two hundred and fifteen days, fourteen hours, twenty seven minutes, and forty two seconds, using current transportation."

"I'd be happy just to see another human," Jeff sighed in disgust. He hesitated as he thought about Lori for a second or two. He began to miss her again.

"I'm sure your friend Lori is fine," Zarcon assured him as he read his thoughts.

"Would you mind not reading my mind?" Jeff requested, a bit annoyed.

"Forgive me, Mr. Walker, I didn't mean to offend. Do you have another question for the computer?"

"Yea. How is it possible for the Tolarions to move from one dimension to the next so swiftly?"

"I can answer that," Zarcon said to enlighten him. "They have improved the device to an extent, but it's not perfected, and is still highly unstable. They could be transferring to another universe and create a void between universes behind them, trapping any other vessel in it. The ship could implode from the enormous pressure placed upon it if the wormhole collapses. The Republic knows how to perform this operation safely. Time and space travel are not matters to be taking lightly."

"Which is why I came here," Jeff said. "I was hoping that you could tell me how they found me so quickly?"

"Are you aware that each of their ships has a homing device?" Zarcon asked. They left the room and walked down another corridor until they came to two sliding doors. They opened as Jeff turned towards him.

"No," he answered. "Well how come they haven't captured us yet?"

"Maybe the device is no longer functioning, or they are waiting to see what your next move is, who knows? At any rate, I'll have it dismantled so they can't

29

follow you any longer. If they've lightened up at all, it's because they are toying with you. If you ask me, I think you ought to wait to leave. The Tolarions are extremely powerful, and unless you catch them off-guard, as you have in the past, they have the upper hand. You were fortunate enough to get three of their craft without being attacked. They will not let you do that again. I suggest waiting for one of their attacks. Then you can disrupt them at their source-the main control center on the planet Tolaria."

"Where is that?" Jeff asked, as they entered a room containing large nuclear fusion turbines.

"This is our main power source," Zarcon said, as he evaded the question for a moment. "It manages the entire power of this base and city. It runs on three fusion reactor chambers, which are located below us. This entire city can be converted into a spacecraft if there is a major disaster."

"You didn't answer my question."

"Very well, Mr. Walker. If you must know, you'll find the Tolarion base at the edge of this galaxy. It will take approximately four weeks Mars time to get there from here, depending where you emerge from the wormhole."

"Have they ever attacked this planet?"

"No, not yet. We can be a formidable enemy when we want to be. Let's continue our tour, shall we?" Jeff was bothered by his appearance considerably; his large protruding mandibles clicking but not speaking, the two large blue compound eyes staring down at him with an emptiness in them, and the long four arms and claws that could break his hand with one snip, and his uncertainty if he could trust him or not. He never had a conversation with an insect before, let alone one that was able to read his thoughts.

After they visited the power room, they ventured through the remainder of the complex. He was completely bewildered by their architecture; everything was made of shiny silver steel, and shaped in ways he never thought possible. Their city under a dome had a style of it own, totally alien to anything on Earth or Mars. He firmly believed if they were attacked, they would only sustain minimal damage. Towards the end of his tour, Zarcon came to a room marked 'investigative research.' They entered it and the doors shut behind them.

"This is why the Tolarions will not attack us," he replied, as he waved his claw like hand. "In this room are some of the most devastating devices you will ever see. We don't like war, but in a universe of violent races it becomes necessary to protect ourselves from those which mean to harm us."

He walked over to two doors on the far side of the large room and pressed a button on a panel that opened them. They revealed a large thirty feet weapon pointed out into space; its tip extended through the roof of the large dome in the ceiling, similar to a planetarium. It had several sections on it and went into larger sections until it reached the base. Jeff gathered that this was so it could retract into itself for it to be more compact. He had no idea as to exactly what it was, but he knew it wasn't just to say hello to their neighbors.

"We call it the Belorion death ray," the insect explained. "It's the only one of its kind in either of our universes. It is capable of destroying an entire planet anywhere in this galaxy just by operating the controls in the briefing room next door." This proved to Jeff their intentions were not peaceful. Maybe it was just a gut feeling, but Jeff was skeptical, and didn't trust their rhetoric.

"Why would beings of peace such as yourselves create such a thing?"

"Deterrence, my friend, deterrence. Life is a precious commodity. It doesn't matter if someone is constructive or destructive; they still deserve to live. Surely as humans have made mistakes on your own planet you understand that by using it, we would make a grave mistake. There is no reason to destroy the Tolarions until they become a serious threat."

"You don't consider them a serious threat? When will they become one, after they take over half the galaxy?"

"Until now, they have only been gaming with us, watching us carefully. We are at a stalemate with them, but if we could get somebody on the inside-"

"You mean to tell me that the Tolarions have this weapon too?"

"I've only heard rumors that they have spies here. I have no evidence yet. Is it possible that maybe you could help us with a little mission of our own?"

"We're all outsiders to all this!" Jeff barked. He wanted no part of their battle with the Tolarions, and he couldn't figure out why they wanted him of all people. "We just landed here because we felt it was a safe place to land, not get involved in an intergalactic war!"

"I understand what you're saying, but if they have stolen the plans to the death ray, it could be the end of life as we know it for all of us," Zarcon remarked. "You said that you destroyed three of their ships, and you obviously stole one as well. After the tracking device is removed, and our own tracking system is installed, it will be impossible for them to find you. It's similar to what you call a jamming device."

"We can't fight them alone!" Jeff pleaded with the Belorion.

"Of course not. We'll help you. You'll be accompanied by your friends, my best analyst and a security crew will follow you in another craft. I would assist you myself, but I have my duties here." They exited the room and started down the hallway. "I'm having a banquet for the Republic committee tonight," he stated. As a spokesman for the human race, I think you should attend. Perhaps your friends would also like to attend representing their small planet?"

"Yes, of course," Jeff answered. "We'd be honored."

Two guards approached Zarcon as they saluted. Jeff felt a little uneasy about the whole situation, but he felt now he could trust them after knowing a little more. "Show our guest to his quarters, and bring him anything he wants," Zarcon said. He turned to Jeff. "I'm sure you're as anxious to learn about us as we are about you. There is a computer in your quarters that will be of some use to you. I will contact you when dinner is about to begin."

He nodded, and followed the guards to the end of the corridor until they came to a room on the right. The room wasn't very large, and the only items in it were two beds, two chairs, a small table, and a computer implanted into the wall. Dormiton approached Jeff, who waited diligently for the aliens to leave the room. Jeff held his finger to his lips, and searched the room for hidden microphones or cameras. He found nothing noticeable to the naked eye. As the Belorions exited the room and started down the hallway, the door slid shut behind them.

"Well," his amphibian friend asked. "What do you think?"

"I don't know," he answered.

"They seem peaceful enough. They took Milgic down to be treated. They said he'd be on his feet by dinner."

"I think we should be cautious. I know they seem peaceful, but they have instruments of violence. I've seen one of their weapons, and they're just as bad as the Tolarions. It seems that they're currently at war with them, and neither side is capable of winning without destroying the other. They have a gun capable of wiping out an entire planet. I don't like it!"

"What do you suggest we do then?"

"We'll have to go along with them until we can find out what their motives really are. We're all invited to a banquet tonight. Maybe we can get some answers there." Having not rested for a day and a half, he slept quite comfortably for a few hours. When he awoke, Dormiton was lost in concentration. "What are you thinking about?" Jeff asked, yawning.

"About what happened on Lingwort. Why did they kill our people, we didn't do anything to them? All we wanted was peace."

"And all they wanted was conquest," Jeff stated, as he stretched and sat up in the bed. His tone was firm, but he tried to consider the amphibian's point of view. "Look, Dormiton-you made a choice. You had to choose between running and making a stand. You'll soon find that most places aren't like Lingwort. Sometimes you have to fight for your freedom! If you're blaming yourself for your friends' deaths, don't. It wasn't your fault. If you must blame someone, blame your enemies that brought this upon you."

"I will kill no one, and blame no one. There has been enough bloodshed already. We should not get involved."

"We're already involved, whether you like it or not! We're going to have to come up with a plan of our own." He was interrupted by the voice of the intercom calling his name. He pressed a red transmitter button.

"This is Walker," he answered.

"This is Zarcon. The banquet is to begin shortly. There are two guards outside your quarters. They will escort you to the briefing room."

"Thank you," Jeff answered. "We will be there shortly." He turned off the transmitter and the door opened. They followed the guards as they were instructed until they came to a large room with three tables at its center. There were ten chairs at each of them, eating utensils, plates, and glasses at each place setting. The glasses were an uneven peculiar design he never saw before.

Zarcon was already in the room, and greeted them at the door. "Make yourselves comfortable, gentlemen," he said. They walked over to where their friend Milgic was. He was much better, and fully alert. Zarcon addressed the guards as the guests seated themselves. "Have the Republic members arrived yet?"

"Yes, Sir," one of them answered. "They are on their way up now. The ambassador of Zeloria refused to meet our advisors, however."

"That is unfortunate," their leader sighed and shook his head. "And I was so sure that they would be on their way to peace. They refuse to believe that the Tolarions are a threat to them, typical human characteristics." Jeff was a little offended by this remark but tried to stay on the topic of the conversation anyway.

"The Zelorion people are human beings?" he asked.

"They're human beings, all right," he answered. "They are primitive, savage, arrogant humans. They refuse to accept policies that would only benefit them, and are currently trading weapons with the Tolarions. If they refuse to listen to us, the Tolarions will take their planet. We have tried to become their allies, but they accuse us of interfering. We have no other alternative than to discontinue our conferences with them."

"You would just let the Tolarions invade them?"

"Well there is nothing else we can do. We've tried deploying troops there, but it's getting so you don't know who is fighting whom. The Republic suggests that there be no further interference, and I willing to go along with that. Let their own ignorance be their undoing."

"You can't save lives by condemning them!" Jeff said. "The Republic doesn't decide for everybody, does it?"

"Who is this?" a voice interrupted. All eyes were fixed upon the door. A guest who arrived was disturbed by his words. He was an alien, resembling a humanoid, but had long sharp black nails at the end of his fingers. He wore no masks, so he obviously could breathe Oxygen as well. He had no body or facial hair, was white in complexion, and his red eyes were narrow, and were black around his eyelids. Unlike Zarcon who used thoughts, he actually spoke English. Again, this surprised Jeff. "A native of Zeloria, perhaps?"

"No, Riona," Zarcon answered. "This is Jeff Walker, an inhabitant of a planet called Mars. He and his friends came here in a spaceship they stole from the Tolarions. He believes that we should defend Zeloria, rather than choose not to interfere."

"Nonsense!" the humanoid barked. "If we do that, we would jeopardize our own resources. They must combine their forces with the Republic for their own protection. That will not be possible if they continue to buy weapons off our enemies."

"I see your point," Jeff stated. "But I think you should help them anyway. Perhaps if a human were to talk with them-"

"Being human yourself, you should know that they would kill you as a spy,"

33

Riona laughed. "No, Mr. Walker, it would be best for you to stay out of affairs that don't concern you."

Jeff was willing to cooperate, but he was growing impatient with his mind games. "Zarcon invited me as his guest!" Jeff said. "My friends' home planet has been attacked; my home planet has been attacked, possibly by these Tolarions! Not to mention that I've been chased halfway across two universes by them, and you tell me that it doesn't concern me? I'd like to know what someone is going to do about this situation."

"You," Riona sneered. "Shall do nothing. Zarcon was wrong to invite you to this private conference. You are not a member of the Republic. It is in the Republic's hands, as it will always be. I suggest you leave before the other members arrive."

"And if I refuse?"

"If you do anything to prevent our agenda, then you may find your life considerably shorter, my friend!" From his dark blue cloak that resembled a friar or monk's, he pulled out a laser and pointed at Jeff. The guards prevented the other guests from entering during the incident.

"Is this your idea of peace?" Jeff asked, as he watched the laser in his hand close. Two guards' headbands glowed brightly as they approached him. He stared at Zarcon in distrust, but he just waved his four arms as if he knew nothing of Riona's actions.

"Zarcon!" Riona yelled in anger. "You were a fool for allowing these intruders here! It's obvious that they are siding with the Zelorions and are spies! I'm holding you personally responsible for this outrage and you will pay the penalty!"

He pointed his gun towards the insect, but Jeff kicked it from his hand, knocking it to the floor. Before he was able to grab it, Riona waved his arm, and sent Jeff across the room against the far wall. Riona held open his hand, and the laser seemed to fly into it. The human couldn't believe what he was seeing; telekinesis was impossible as far as he knew.

"Do you really believe you can hurt me?" he laughed. "I have twice your physical strength, Human, and five times your mental strength. You are no match for me! Guards, take these intruders and President Zarcon to the brig. Tomorrow they will be brought to Sentros for trial. I am assuming command of this planet until further notice. It will be my personal pleasure to see you executed Zarcon. I always knew you were a traitor to the Galactic Republic."

The crowd of ambassadors in the hallway stared at their leader in astonishment as the prisoners were pushed through the doors. He couldn't believe his own people treated him this way. When they reached the brig, the same officer who earlier followed Zarcon's orders now shoved him inside the room. He held his four arms out to his guests in sympathy. "Why is it that when I question orders I am punished?" he asked. "If I agree to help you, they accuse me of being a spy. You are no more spies than I am the leader of Tolaria. There is something going on here, but I can quite put a 'finger on it', as you humans say, but in my case that would be a claw."

"It doesn't feel right to me either," Jeff replied. "Why doesn't the Republic want to intervene with Zeloria?"

"Probably because Riona is right. To help them would be senseless. They would only turn their weapons against us. They have been siding with the Tolarions for years."

"How do you know that?" Dormiton asked. He didn't fully understand this thing called 'war', but he was beginning to. "Have you ever been there?"

"Of course not," Zarcon answered.

"Then how do you know they are in league with the Tolarions?" Jeff asked. "Maybe it's a propaganda stunt by the Republic to get your race to hate them. Maybe they have a hidden agenda that you're unaware of?"

"That is highly unlikely," Zarcon replied.

"There's always that possibility," Jeff said. "We'll never know by staying here. We have to find a way out."

Jeff paced the room as he thought of an escape strategy. Zarcon and the lingworts eyed each other over carefully, still not fully trusting one another. Jeff turned to the large insect. "What are the headbands for?" Jeff asked, as he watched it faintly illuminate. "A weapon?"

"No, it's my thought translator," he explained. "It allows us to communicate with other beings such as yourselves. It is essential that we try to open relations with all forms of life."

"Where do they keep the weapons here?" Jeff asked, still focused on escape.

"There are no hand held weapons, as you are thinking, Mr. Walker," he answered. "Our weapon is the mind, which in some ways can be more effective. Our spaceships, however, are armed with photonic lasers, as yours is as well."

"Considering that we're all about to be executed, you can skip the formalities and call me Jeff," the human remarked. "What happens if two minds fight each other?"

"The stronger one wins, of course."

"Who has the stronger mind, you or the guard?"

"I do, but Riona is here, and if we escape he will know."

"He is not a Belorion, how can his mind be so strong?"

"No, he is not," explained the insect. "He is from a planet long dead. He is also the President of the council of the Galactic Republic, unfortunately."

"No wonder he speaks so highly of it," Milgic added.

"When did he acquire this power?" Jeff asked.

"No one knows," Zarcon remarked. "We just know that he has too powerful a mind to suppress. He is in charge, and if you disobey him, then you suffer the consequences."

"We'll worry about him when the time comes," Jeff said. "We have to at least try. Can you get the guard to deactivate the force field?"

"You like to live dangerously, don't you, Human?" Zarcon asked.

"Can you get them to open the door," he repeated.

"Yes, but we'll be captured the minute we get to the spaceship, if not before," Zarcon said, doubtful, as the guards turned their heads towards the four of them.

"Can you keep Riona occupied until we can make it to the ship?" Jeff asked.

"I can try, but he'll probably kill me and come after you. He is very powerful."

"And I am very persistent," Jeff remarked. "We have to at least give it a try. We're going to die anyway and I for one am not looking forward to being executed."

The force field was deactivated, and Riona entered the room, aware of their whole attempt at a plan. "I underestimated you, Mr. Walker," he announced. "You're much more defiant than I expected. It won't happen again, I assure you."

"If you know what I'm thinking than you know I'm telling the truth about Mars," Jeff said. Riona walked over to him, his face just inches away from his own.

"I know that," he whispered, raising his right index nail to Jeff's throat and narrowing his evil red eyes. "As you may know by now, I'm not all that I appear to be. Being leader of the Galactic Republic has given me certain advantages, including executing anyone I see fit. No one can defy my powers. I just thought that you wouldn't catch on to me so quickly. Justice has to be served, my foolish friend, and your primitive human brain is no match for mine. I've arranged a presentation for you and my dear old friend Zarcon, I hope you enjoy it. Guards, take them to the viewing room."

"What are you up to?" Jeff hissed as he stepped forwards, only to be intercepted by two of the guards. Riona then turned to Zarcon.

"Trying to test my mind, Zarcon?" he laughed. "Shame on you. Test this!" He waved his hand which lifted Zarcon in the air and threw him against the far wall, bumping his head, and rendering him unconscious. Dormiton stepped in, only to be stopped by Milgic. The guards picked up Zarcon from the floor and dragged him from the room. Riona pointed the laser at the others.

"Let's go," he snapped, as he backed up and kept his distance. They were led down the hallway to a briefing room. Jeff couldn't quite understand why someone as powerful as him insisted on using a laser. Perhaps he only had limited power over what he could do with his mind

"Your friend Zarcon will be fine," Riona said, as he read Jeff's mind. He wanted to do something, but with Riona's extraordinary abilities, he found it difficult to escape. They were guided into the viewing room and instructed to sit down. There was a large viewing screen in its center, as well as a computer panel. Zarcon began to come out of his daze. "I know that our friend Zarcon here gave away classified information to you, Mr. Walker. "It makes no difference that his intentions were harmless. I have no way of knowing you are who you say you are.

36

Spies have come before me, trying to successfully block my thought patterns. You have all committed treason. What is the sentence for treason, Zarcon?" He raised his head, still somewhat dazed, but aware of what was happening.

"Death," he said.

"That is correct, my friend," Riona jeered and pressed some buttons on the panel. "There are billions and billions of stars in this galaxy and in your own universe. We can destroy any planet that orbits them just by pushing a series of coordinates. The Galactic republic is trying to negotiate a peaceful and profitable coexistence with most planets, regardless of their own personal interests. However, we cannot condone a society of humans who insist on aiding our enemies. Now I have two choices- I can either destroy Zeloria, which will surely start an unavoidable war with the Tolarions, or I can destroy your puny little red planet, Mr. Walker. What is it going to be?"

"What do you want from me?" Jeff asked, puzzled.

"The truth, Mr. Walker, the truth," he sneered with an evil grin. Jeff tried to keep his mind off the location of the Mars base the best he could, but found it extremely difficult. Riona approached him and pressed the laser against his temple. "Try to defy me, and I'll blow your head off!"

Jeff didn't want to see any planet destroyed, but he also didn't want his own race obliterated either, assuming that the Tolarions hadn't retaliated and destroyed it already. Why did Balta and Riona have such an interest in where Mars was anyways? His only alternative was to bluff him.

"Just to show you how human I am," he joked. "You can go ahead and destroy my planet."

Riona smiled, as he anticipated his behavior. "No, I don't think so," he said. "The Federation has had just enough of Zeloria, so I choose Zeloria. Goodbye, Traitors."

He entered the proper coordinates for the planet, and a bluish-green world appeared on the viewing screen. He pressed a button on the panel, which activated the death ray at the helpless planet. They watched in anguish, as the world exploded, sending fragments across space and the viewing screen. Over fifty million lives were lost instantly. The Tolarions would probably find out about it, if they hadn't already. If Zarcon was telling the truth about Riona's powers, and the capabilities of this new weapon, they'd better prepare to meet their match in any universe.

CHAPTER FOUR

After the last particles of the planet disbanded into the darkness of space, Riona turned towards the human. He pressed another button which closed the screen doors. He raised his right index claw again, and approached Jeff, more solemn than before.

"You don't understand me, do you, Mr. Walker?" he asked. "I am not a violent being, and I don't like war, but sometimes there is no other way. I am only trying to do what is best for the Republic, as you are trying to do what is best for Tolaria."

"I'm from Mars, not Tolaria."

"You're a liar! Mars is a cold and barren world. There are no humans there!"

"Something must have happened to them," Jeff said. "Maybe the Tolarions attacked them."

"Perhaps, "Riona pondered. "Or maybe you are trying to block it from your memory?"

"Only you would know," Jeff joked.

"True," Riona answered, as he smiled again.

"Release my friends at least!" Jeff pleaded with him. "They have done nothing."

"You will all be executed in good time!" he yelled and became more psychotic, physically slamming Jeff against the wall, grabbing him tight around the neck. "Do you know what type of atmosphere is outside? It is much like your own. It is totally poiseness and unbearable. What better way to kill you than to let you suffocate in a soup of noxious gas! Enough sentimentality, it's time to die!" Jeff crouched, short of breath as the guards lifted him and began towards the door.

"Isn't there any other way?" Zarcon pleaded.

"No, Zarcon," he stated. "You know the Republic is firm on such matters."

While he grabbed Jeff, Zarcon caught Riona off guard, and used his mind to inflict pain on two of the guards. Riona turned towards the commotion, and Jeff grabbed his hand, firing the laser into his leg, which caused Riona to fall to the floor in pain

"Run!" Zarcon yelled to his friends, transmitting brain waves that pierced through Riona's head painfully. When Riona was near unconsciousness, Zarcon ran behind his friends into the corridor. Riona regained his strength, and lifted himself up. Even though Zarcon had maimed him, he was still quite powerful.

Terror flowed through their bloodstreams while they approached the hangar deck. When they entered the Rigil Four, a guard tried to grab Jeff from behind but

Zarcon counteracted his attempt by using his mind. They entered the craft and prepared for take-off. Jeff fired up their propulsion system and the ship began to propel down the hangar deck, and left the dome city, as several Belorians chased after the craft, leaving a path of blue flames behind them as the hangar doors closed behind them.

"How powerful is Riona's mind?" Jeff asked, as they accelerated through the atmosphere and towards space.

"Not powerful enough to do us any harm once we get away from them," Zarcon answered. "I can feel him trying to attack my mind, but his influence is getting weaker."

"Thank God for miracles!" Jeff barked, as the lingworts smiled at him. "Dormiton, switch that red button on the panel. The one that activates the gravity control onboard the ship." His friend responded to his request.

Zarcon glanced at the viewing screen as they approached space. "Republic ships closing at 79,000 parsecs," he stated. "We also have Tolarion ships closing in at 120,000 parsecs."

"Looks like we've outstayed our welcome on both sides of the fences," Jeff said. "Zarcon, you didn't by any chance get time to have your men put the jamming device in, did you?"

"With Riona coming?" he answered. "Their minds were probably under his control the whole time."

"Well then," Jeff answered. "It's gonna take some ingenuity and quick maneuvering to get out of this one. Dorm, activate the dimensional transporter on my command. Zarcon, do the shields need to be on when you travel through the wormhole?"

"Yes," he answered. "But if any those ships get into the field of the portal, they will be with us on the way out."

"Then we'll just have to get them to come after each other. Dorm, how close are they now?"

"Republic ships at 40,000, Tolarion at 80, 000," he answered. "They're activating their weapons system. Impact in eight seconds." Three seconds passed and Jeff responded.

"Now," he yelled. "Get us out of here, Dorm!" He pressed the button, and within seconds, a solar flare appeared again from the closest sun intersecting with the ship's light beam and forming a wormhole, which they passed through and found themselves in any empty quadrant of space.

"Where are we?" the amphibian asked, feeling a bit dazed again.

"Back in Mr. Walker's own universe," Zarcon stated. "Somewhere in the Orion system. We cannot stay here long; they will find us. We've got to find a place to hide and come up with a plan."

"I agree," Jeff answered. The lingworts looked at each other like their friends were insane. All this jumping in space was making them feel like they had rolled down a hill.

"Are you two out of your minds?" Dormiton screeched. "A plan to do what? How do you expect us to go up against both sides? We'll be killed!"

"If we don't do something we're as good as dead anyway," Jeff replied.

"You are willing to die for this senseless war?" Milgic asked.

"They've probably killed off both our races already. What else do you suggest we do," Jeff asked the amphibians.

"Survive," Dormiton answered. "If what you say is true, we are the last of our races and we must preserve that legacy." He admired the fact that he finally was catching onto the idea of optimistic thinking.

"I don't intend on dying yet," Jeff said. "But we can't allow Riona to go through with his plans of using that death ray."

"Well," Milgic muttered. "You can count me out of any plans you have."

"Well, at any rate," interrupted Zarcon. "We have to find a place to hide. I'll send out a probe." He pressed a button, which launched a tiny probe into the darkness ahead of them.

The computer relayed its findings to the crew of the Rigil Four. "Nearest planet is Zebula. Two weeks arrival at maximum speed," it said. "Oxygen-nitrogen atmosphere, surface temperature 90 degrees at equator, approximately 72% water. Land masses at the North and South poles and at the equator. No intelligent life forms present."

"Set course for Zebula, maximum speed. Keep shields down, unless enemy ships are indicated." Jeff was curious to find out a little more about the Tolarion government so he consulted the computer. "Computer," Jeff commanded. "Tell me more about these Tolarions."

"The Tolarions evolved as a race 105 years ago," the computer responded. "They are a race of genetically altered humanoid, developed from simian, human, and an undefined alien DNA by the 21st century human Tolarion leader, Akros."

Jeff digested the information, amazed to believe that a human had anything to do with this grotesque race of beings or with wormholes for that manner. This explained why they were able to understand English. He remembered from Earth history one particular man had gone farther on the study of genes than others, but he found himself unable to remember his name. The other question he had was how this particular human would know anything about theories that weren't even developed on Earth or Mars yet.

"How did the human reach Tolaria?" Jeff asked.

"Insufficient data," it answered.

"What was his name?"

"Insufficient data."

"What is the location of Tolaria and its known defense systems in relation to its own universe?"

"Tolaria is in star sector 18-905 in the Aria star system. Defense systems unavailable to this unit," the machine answered. He became impatient with the device. He began to wonder if the alleged attack on Mars wasn't a deliberate attack to get humans involved with the conflict. They wanted to rule every planet in both universes, and the humans were just as much a threat to them as Riona.

"How did the Tolarions develop the ability to travel through wormholes?" the human asked.

"Insufficient data," the computer evasively stated again.

While Dormiton periodically monitored the scanners, Jeff consulted the computer one more time about a connection between the three worlds of Earth, Beloria, and Tolaria. They all were similar in composition, but their atmospheric characteristics were different. Earth was mostly nitrogen-oxygen based, Tolaria was mostly nitrous oxide, and Beloria was mostly carbon-dioxide. Oxygen was present in each atmosphere, but the concentration of each one was different.

Something else was odd. They received readings of a distress call from Beloria which was recorded before they left the other universe. It couldn't have been a Tolarion attack because the Republic sensors would have detected this. Two thoughts passed through his mind-either the Republic set a trap for them, or he suspected something more sinister was going on.

"Is it possible for your planet's defenses to have a malfunction?" he asked Zarcon.

"Not likely. The Tolarions must have attacked."

"No, I don't think so," Jeff said. "I've got a bad feeling that something else has gone terribly wrong. Well, at any rate, we can't turn back."

"Our lives are in your hands, Captain Walker," Zarcon said.

He liked the sound of 'captain.' He always wanted his own starship to command, but not under these stressful circumstances. He only flew small scout ships that surveyed close to uninhabitable worlds that tormented the soul. He didn't realize at the time the size of the ship he would later command was much larger than even this one. He allowed Zarcon to pilot the craft while he slept on their journey towards Zebula. He'd been through one of the toughest weeks of his life, and was exhausted. Dormiton and Milgic remained awake with Zarcon, mesmerized by the stars, and began to fully realize how vast space can be.

"I always thought that Lingwort was it," Dormiton said to his life-long friend. "To think, we're only one kind of animal among billions in this emptiness called 'space.'"

"Will we ever see home again?" Milgic asked.

"Probably not. Once we left there, I don't think Jeff had any intentions on going back."

"I wonder what happened to the rest of our people."

"They are probably all right. That is if the Tolarions didn't get them."

"I don't like this thing called 'war.' It has separated us from our homeland, and brought out bitterness in Jeff."

"Yes, I know. He used to be a lot happier."

"Until the aliens came."

"Yes the aliens. Milgic, would it be wrong to feel anger over the loss of our friends?"

"I think I can answer that," Zarcon interrupted. "If you feel the Tolarions are responsible for their deaths, then you are not wrong. Although it is not always advisable to fight for what you believe is right, sometimes you have no choice. This is what we call 'war.'"

"Why can't we just find a planet to live on in peace?" Milgic asked.

"Because the Tolarions will not allow us to do so. They'll keep on invading worlds until somebody stops them. Right now we just have to bide our time until we come up with a plan."

"How can the four of us defeat an empire?" screeched Milgic, who almost woke Jeff up. He rolled over, and went back to sleep.

"We alone cannot," Zarcon explained. "But we can find other worlds willing to join our cause."

"Like the world we're going to?" Milgic asked.

"No, there isn't any advanced life there. We're going there to seek refuge until we can figure out what to do."

"Will we be safe there?" Dormiton inquired.

"For a while," Zarcon said. "I have to work on a jamming device so the Tolarions cannot detect us. The Galactic Republic won't be as easy to escape from, however. Their ships are just as fast as this one, and we cannot hide from Riona's powers. He knows everything about the Tolarions and the Republic's defense systems."

"He does?" Jeff asked, just awaking from his long rest. "That explains a little. Is it possible that he is a double-agent?"

"You're joking," Zarcon stated. "He's the president of the council!"

"Which gives him full access to all information, correct?"

"That is correct," Zarcon answered, seeing his point. He also now saw that something much more sinister was going on than just an attack or invasion. Someone in the council lied to him, and he was going to get to the bottom of it sooner or later. "You don't suppose he's used the fusion ray again do you?"

"Let's hope not," Jeff said. "But it kind of appears that way. Why don't you explain to me how it works?"

"The gun is fired by a nuclear fusion based generator in its base that can absorb the amount of energy needed from a nearby sun, and then distributes it to its target wherever that may be. It is also capable of generating a wormhole if necessary to achieve the task."

"Again I ask," the human inquired. "Why the hell would you create such a thing? You people sure like to play with fire!"

They obtained every piece of information they could extract from the ship's computer banks, including the location of their main control center and weapons arsenal on the planet of Tolaria. Zarcon did the best he could on a jamming device but he lacked certain materials he needed. He lacked Cobalt to finish the casing on it, and there was none on the ship. He was certain he could find it on Zebula.

With the planet only a few days away, they prepared themselves for whatever animal life was there. Zarcon was more of a scientist than a diplomat, and was eager to study it. Jeff warned him, however, to keep any life forms away from the ship, and to carry a weapon with him just in case they were hostile.

Dormiton and Milgic were ordered to stay on board after their arrival. They were trapped inside the vessel for a long while and were starting to get edgy with one another. "I need someone to watch the ship," Jeff explained to them. "We can't afford to risk all of our lives!"

"If there are dangerous animals what do we do?" Milgic asked.

"Stay in the ship!" Jeff answered. "Even if I'm killed in the process."

"What if we're captured?"

"I don't have all the answers, Guys," Jeff said. "Chances are we will not get killed if we're careful. Isn't that right, Zarcon?"

"Yes, that is correct," he answered.

"What will this world be like?" asked Dormiton. "Will we able to swim in it?"

"I don't know," Jeff said. "I don't even know if we can drink the water, let alone swim in it."

"I hope so," Milgic replied. "I hope it's filled with beautiful trees and white sandy beaches, just like Lingwort."

"That's very doubtful," Zarcon stated. "Sensors indicate that the vegetation is limited and only in certain regions."

"Well, Zarcon, let's aim for one of those regions," Jeff instructed. "We're all very hungry and tired. Hopefully there will edible vegetation there."

"You do not eat meat?" Zarcon asked the human, surprised.

"I do, but my friends don't."

"Don't they eat insects like most amphibians?"

"Their ancestors once did. Their culture has taught them that it's wrong to kill, even for food." Zarcon nodded, and checked the scanners again.

Ten days passed since their departure from the other universe, and there was still no sign of enemy craft. They knew their luck wouldn't last forever, and they were beginning to get a little nervous. Zarcon eyed the scanners and the lingworts stayed alert in case they were needed. "Still no sign of Riona," Zarcon stated. "We've been lucky."

"What's so lucky about two days without food?" grumbled Milgic.

"Well," Jeff said. "Let's not press our luck. We've still got to make it to Zebula in one piece once we get there, however, it will be difficult to leave without being attacked."

"Not if I can finish the jamming device in time," Zarcon added.

"If we have time to finish it. Besides, you even said yourself that it would not be effective against your own people."

"Yes, that is true. The only way to defeat him is with the mind," Zarcon said.

He turned back to the scanner console. The probe sent back more

44

information about the aquatic world. "Sensors indicate that there are reptilian life forms on Zebula."

"Reptilian?" asked the commander.

"Yes, reptilian."

"Any indication of size and anatomical structure?"

"Not at this time."

"Send out another probe."

"There is only one left. If we use that, we have no indication that there may be life on other worlds."

"Well then," Jeff stated. "We only have one other choice. We'll have to land and hope for the best. We'll have to probably still hijack another Tolarion ship for supplies at some point." The two lingworts looked at each other in disgust and disbelief, and Dormiton put his hand over his face and shook his head.

"That may be difficult," Zarcon said. "They seldom travel alone."

"Why don't you find a hole and bury yourself deeper?" shouted Dormiton. "Why can't we just land and hide until they're gone?"

"We're not sure we'll even be able to," Jeff answered.

By the next morning, they were only an hour or two away from their destination. As the time passed, they faintly saw the bluish green world, slightly larger than Earth and orbiting a small yellow sun. Its two moons shined brightly towards the star as the renegades' ship passed by them. The two lingworts stared at the world in wonder, and Jeff knew in his mind their thoughts were on home. They didn't want any part of the situation; they just wanted to be left alone in an environment they could live peacefully.

"We're coming up on Zebula now," Zarcon stated, as peered in his scanners.

"Reduce engines to orbital speed," the leader told the computer. It followed the order and the ship's engines slowed down. "Any sign of enemy craft?"

"None," Zarcon answered, a little bewildered why Riona hadn't found them yet.

"Good," Jeff said. "Prepare to enter the atmosphere. Shields on; fire reverse thrust."

They approached the surface, and Jeff directed the ship towards the equatorial land-mass. There were many mountains and desert regions upon the land, but he didn't see much in the way of vegetation, only in scattered areas. He figured they better land before any Republic vessels picked them up on their sensors. They entered a canyon, in which there was a river running through it. There was some foliage along its edges, in the form of brush and trees. He switched the velocity to sub orbital speed and landed along the dry embankment of the river. It was a little tricky to land in such a narrow space, but he was successful. Dust flew everywhere until the ship firmly set on the ground. He turned to Zarcon once they landed.

"Everyone will stay on board until I say it's safe, understand?" They all nodded. "Are there still readings of reptilian life?"

"Yes," Zarcon answered.

"Any signs of whether they're primitive or advanced?"

"Not at this time."

Jeff grabbed a laser pistol, some supplies, his backpack, and headed for the main door hatch. "Zarcon," he said, turning towards him. "I want you to stay here with the other two. If there's hostile life out there, I don't want us all to get killed. You can do your scientific observations after we know what we're dealing with. Luckily we landed near a river. I'll bring back some water with me. It is safe to drink?"

"Yes," Zarcon answered.

"If I'm not back in three hours, you can look for me, but only you. I don't want our ship to fall into enemy hands." He nodded, as Jeff hit the main door controls. He held his laser tight as it slid open, and revealed the earth-like gorge that surrounded him, and the bright blue sky and the shadows that silhouetted the rocks around him.

Jeff jumped out, and felt the sandy soil beneath his boots. He started to follow the river embankment that flowed about six miles to the south, according to his hand held locating device. Judging from the vegetation in the area, the world didn't appear to support dinosaurs. He surmised the reptiles picked up by the sensors were probably snakes or lizards. That would explain why the probe didn't pick them up clearly. The sensors were designed to detect life forms, but only on the surface and not underneath.

Jeff embraced the full beauty of this livable, likable world. The sound of the river was extremely tempting, and he couldn't resist going for a swim. He set his laser gun down and hid it beneath his suit he took off. Completely naked, he jumped into the cool and refreshing water. He knew he needed to be careful, but the alluring appeal of the river was too hard to resist. The river's current was just strong enough to make it difficult to stand. This didn't bother Jeff because he was an excellent swimmer, swimming quite frequently in the artificial lakes on Mars and the ocean on Lingwort.

After Jeff bathed and drank a canteen full of it, he submerged some extra canteens underwater. He put his suit back on, picked up his laser gun, and started back to the ship to the others. He decided to investigate after he heard a startling sound up the river. It was as if something was watching him through the woods. He dropped the canteens in the sand, raised his laser gun, threw on his pack, and headed south following the river embankment.

The temperature felt around eighty degrees to him and was quite comfortable. He guessed they arrived in the spring months due the fact that the foliage was green. The forest nearby budded leaves, and the river was high but not overflowing the embankment. Jeff also heard the sound of the birds in the distance, but this was not the sound he heard a few minutes before.

It was a long time since he actually felt water that wasn't salty or stagnant, other than the waterfall or springs on the island. Jeff also breathed the air here

46

easier. He found many times the air on Lingwort wasn't to his liking because it was thinner. He began to wonder why he ever wanted to get back to Mars in the first place. If his suspicions were true, there was really nothing left for him anyways.

Nonetheless, Mars was where his people were, and if he was wrong, he had to protect them from these invaders from a parallel universe. The idea was so bizarre he had a hard time believing it, but it was really happening. If he told Mars Mission Control there was a race with a weapon that was capable of destroying entire worlds and able to travel through wormholes, they would think he was crazy.

A mile down the river, Jeff came to a lake surrounded by a small jungle. The ravine got rockier, and was part of a mountain ridge that overlooked the lake on its north side. Jeff climbed on some rocks overlooking the area where a waterfall flowed into it, and admired the view of the rain forest for a few moments. He guessed the lake was about two miles long and the forest went on as far as his eyes could see. There was some wreckage near the lake in a small clearing, but it was impossible to determine its identity from such a distance.

Jeff also saw an ocean to the west side, as well as more mountains. It was a breathtaking view a photographer would have died for. He eyed the waterfall below him, and anchored his footing, careful not to slip.

It took Jeff back to a time when his grandfather was still alive. He was twelve when he last saw him on the Martian base. Colonel Thomas J. Walker saw the destruction of Earth firsthand, the rebuilding of society first underground and then on the space stations. He told Jeff the stories his father told him; stories that seemed like ancient fables now. Grandfather Walker used to have a cup of hot chocolate with Jeff and his uncle and talk about the way Earth used to be before the war. None of them saw it personally, but they'd describe it just the same.

Thomas Walker asked his grandchild if he wanted a marshmallow in his chocolate to start the conversation. "Yes please," Jeff said, as he smiled. His uncle and his grandfather raised him since he was eight, when his parents were killed in an explosion.

"Did I ever tell you what you're great grandfather used to tell me?" Thomas asked. "It was in 2045, I was almost your age. He talked about how beautiful the Earth was before the war, how there were great cities with millions of people. This was before we moved underground, before the air strikes."

"How long did people live underground?" Jeff asked, as he sipped his hot chocolate.

"At least thirty years," he said, mimicking his grandchild's action.

"Before that everybody lived above ground," his Uncle Clark added.

"What was that like?" the tween asked.

"Completely different from here," Thomas exclaimed. "The forests weren't in domes and there was an atmosphere to breath."

"Were there rivers, lakes and beaches like in the domes?" Jeff asked.

"Yes," his grandfather continued. "They were much vaster than here. The oceans were so large that it took weeks to get from port to port. The mountains were so large they touched the sky!"

"They touch the sky here," Jeff remarked.

"But you can't climb them here," Clark reminded him.

"What about the forests?"

"There were all kinds of forests," Tom explained. "Rainforests with pine trees, jungles with vines, and swamps. They were like the forest we have here, only bigger."

"What about animals," Jeff asked.

"There was every kind of animal you can think of," his grandfather told him. "There were birds, lizards, raccoons, wolves, kangaroos, and giraffes."

"What are kangaroos and giraffes?" the inquisitive child asked.

"Well," Clark said. "A kangaroo looks a little like a rabbit, but is bigger, has bigger legs and a pouch in its front. They used to live in Australia."

"What about a giraffe?" Jeff asked.

"They have four legs like a horse, have spots, and are about fifteen feet tall," Clark answered.

"Really?"

"Yes, really," Thomas laughed.

He never forgot about those last days he sat with his elderly grandfather, and the days he spoke about working for NASA. They built an underground base prior to the attacks from the Iranians, Iraqis, and the Russians that were safe from nuclear fallout. Thomas Walker was born there, and lived most of his life there until they built the space stations and the Mars base. The governments that were left unified into one organization, the NASA Initiative for Interplanetary Exploration, and it was from this that the Martian Space Academy was born.

As he was lost in deep nostalgia, he felt the pain of something sharp piercing into his back, and then being pushed over the cliff into the raging water. He screamed in pain when he felt the sudden blow of rocks on his back and thighs. It propelled him down the waterfall, his body twisted every inch of the way, and amazingly he survived. Falling into the lake, he desperately gasped for air. When finally reaching calmer waters, he maneuvered himself to shore, dragged his bruised body across the sand, his arm broke, and legs bleeding badly. Jeff, now exhausted lay on the shore, closed his eyes, and slipped into unconsciousness.

CHAPTER FIVE

Three hours passed since their comrade left the spaceship, and they began to worry. Zarcon relieved the other two by telling them Jeff went out to do some exploring and lost track of time. He knew when he read their minds that they didn't believe him. It just wasn't like Jeff to just wander off; he always had a good sense of direction, especially in the jungle, where it was difficult to navigate. He always found north by the direction of the sunset and followed the opposite way back, assuming there was a sunset on this planet.

Zarcon scanned the computer screen for more information on the reptiles of the planet. The sensors picked up stronger signals from a ridge one mile away, and indicated there was increased activity from that direction. They were no longer dormant like they had been earlier, and there was a colony of a least thirty of them.

"The reptiles are getting closer," Zarcon remarked, with a curiosity in his mind. "I still wish I knew the size of them."

"We'll never know by staying in here," the annoyed Milgic snorted. "Can't we go out and get some fresh air?"

"Jeff told us to stay in here until he returned," Zarcon answered.

"If he isn't back by now something must have happened to him," Dormiton stated.

"Not necessarily," Zarcon said, as he tried to calm the amphibians. "He may be getting us some food, or supplies."

"Jeff doesn't make a habit of disappearing, Zarcon," Milgic sniped.

"Calm down everybody," he consoled them. "I told you he might be looking for food."

"Or maybe something is making food out of him," Milgic suggested.

"That is very doubtful," Zarcon explained. "Jeff knows how to take care of himself. Besides, sensors indicate reptilian and animal life forms, but nothing that could eat him. Most of the animals are probably herbivores."

"Herbi-what?" Milgic asked, confused by the term.

"Plant eaters like us," Dormiton explained.

"Why do some animals eat meat?" Milgic asked. "Why do they kill?"

"You shouldn't concern yourself with that right now," Zarcon said. "We have to think about if he doesn't return. Tomorrow morning we will have to look for him, but as for tonight we are staying put. We don't know what type of wildlife is really out there, and if there is something big enough to eat us out there, it is better that only one of us gets killed, instead of all of us. Jeff knows that as well as I."

49

"Why does it have to be Jeff?" Dormiton asked, disturbed by his choice of words. "And how can you be so cold about it?"

"Because he is our leader," Zarcon reminded them. "And I am not being cold, just realistic! We must respect his command, even if he's not here. He would not want us to give our lives for him, would he? He does not seem to be that type of man."

"That's because he's not," Dormiton defensively cried. "He is a sensitive, warm and caring man! He would die himself before he let any harm come to us!"

"My case in point," the scholarly insect stated. "It's settled then. In the morning, I'll search for him. You two stay inside the ship until I return. I'll carry a gun, and I want each of you to have one close by as well."

"But we detest guns," Milgic roared, and began to irritate Zarcon.

"Nevertheless," Zarcon remarked, taking a commanding tone. "You will carry them and use them if needed starting now, is that understood? It's about time you started defending yourselves, instead of relying on others to help you. Where would you be if Jeff never landed on your world?"

"Probably still living in caves," Dormiton said."

"Exactly. The Tolarions don't believe in keeping prisoners, unless they are of use to them, and in a society such as yours, conquest would be inevitable. Jeff has proven to them that humans can be clever adversaries, and worthy of their challenge."

"But if they catch him, won't they kill him," Milgic asked.

"Not necessarily. It's not too often that they come across humans intelligent as he is. They may want to use him."

"For what?" the angered Dormiton asked.

"Who knows? Only the Tolarion government can answer that."

"What do we do about your people?" Milgic asked.

"There is nothing we can do but run. They are more advanced than the Tolarions, and will not give up as easily. They can detect our ship as well, which makes it hard to flee from them."

If the Republic captured Jeff, there was nothing Zarcon could even do for him. His political power exhausted and his own people turned against him, his only hope would be to convince the council of his innocence, but first he had to be able to talk to them.

The night was long and lonely for Milgic, who monitored outside with the helm's scanners. He heard several species of animals through the ship's sensory devices. Nothing sounded or seemed unusual, other than their comrade not returning yet. From what he saw on the viewing screens, the world was much drier than Lingwort. The animal sounds he heard consisted of wolves, birds, and insects. Although it was dark, he did notice something close to the river. The figure was sleek and tall, much like a humanoid, and stood as a biped. He knew it couldn't have been Jeff, due to its size, which was close to eight foot tall.

As it turned towards the ship, Milgic noticed a button on the helm marked 'landing lights.' He pressed it, and the outside lights of the craft turned on, revealing the beast. Milgic gazed at the behemoth in fear, which was a reptilian creature of some kind.

"Zarcon!" he screamed, as the creature wailed in pain and scurried into the woods.

Zarcon woke up, and grabbed his laser gun which lay beside him. "What is it," he asked frantically, as he turned off the landing lights. "Why are these on? We don't want anyone to know we're here!"

"I'm sorry!" the frightened amphibian remarked. "Some kind of creature is outside the ship!"

"Life forms only indicate reptilian and animal life," Zarcon stated.

"It was a creature!" he sneered as Dormiton awoke. "It was three times taller than me and green!"

Zarcon checked his scanners, revealing the reptilian life was very close to them. He consulted the computer for some answers. "Indicate structure of reptilian life forms," he ordered.

"Reptilian life form indicated as Vardicon, found on planets Volarius, Remot, Zebula and Zardick in this galaxy. Atomic structure similar to reptiles and humans. Internal temperatures sixty four degrees Fahrenheit. Non intelligent, nocturnal life form. Physical characteristics indicate evolutionary process is under way."

"What evolutionary process?"

"Unable to determine at this time."

"What is their chemical composition?"

"Hydrogen, Nitrogen, Carbon, Iron, Oxygen, Magnesium, and various other elements."

"What is their size?"

"Sensors indicate they are eight feet in height."

"I told you I saw it," Milgic said, pointing his left index finger at the insect.

"What do they consume," the Belorion asked the machine.

"Sensors indicated that they survive on meat, mainly smaller animals."

"Well that's just great!" Milgic snapped. "They've probably already killed Jeff!"

"Let's not jump to any conclusions," Zarcon stated. "We can't go out there tonight, so we'll start first thing in the morning. They cannot travel in the day, so that will work in our favor. They can't get us in here, but just in case they do, take my laser gun." Milgic reluctantly grabbed the weapon from his hand, as his friends returned to slumber.

When the morning arrived, he was still very much awake. Jeff still remained missing, and their time was growing short. Zarcon estimated that they only had a day to find their friend and the materials they needed to complete their jamming device, before their pursuers found out where they were.

Their immediate leader decided to set out by himself, just in case the

Tolarions showed up before the Republic did. The two lingworts were shown how to use the weapons onboard the spacecraft to protect themselves. There were shields to protect the ship from attack, but unfortunately they wouldn't last forever. He approached the amphibians by the door, threw on a back pack, and grabbed a laser pistol.

"Listen to me," he said, his blue compound eyes staring at them. "If I cannot find Commander Walker, and I do not return within two hours, you must abandon the ship immediately. They'll give up searching if no one is on the ship. There is a black button at the top of the helm panel marked 'self destruct.' Press it, and type in the code 623990456 and then get out of there. You will have about sixty seconds to run clear from the ship."

"Can't we go with you?" Milgic pleaded.

"Absolutely not!" their leader stated. "If our enemies catch up with us, we'll need this ship to get away, and I'll need the two of you to get it started before I get in if necessary. At least if I find Jeff we'll have a better chance. Besides, there is nothing you can do to help but stay here."

"Very well," Dormiton agreed. "You are right, as always. Can we at least go swimming in the river?"

"Yes," Zarcon said. "As long as you go no further. And only one of you at a time."

"We won't," Milgic sneered. "Only one at a time. I understand."

"And you better carry guns. Just because we're hidden doesn't mean we're safe."

"Yes, Sir," Dormiton responded, hesitant to pick up the gun. Milgic followed his actions accordingly.

Zarcon opened the main door of the Rigil Four, and peered outside. "It appears there aren't any enemy forces at the moment," he said. "You are free to swim, but be careful. Remember, only one of you at a time should go in. The other should keep watch. I'll be back in a little while."

The insect jumped from the craft unto the sand. He found several footprints around the ship, but only one set were human. He decided that those were his friend's, and proceeded to follow them. His two other companions watched from the ship until he was out of distance, and also jumped out.

"Shouldn't we follow him?" the inquisitive Milgic suggested.

"You heard what he said," Dormiton answered. "He needs somebody to watch the ship."

"You don't really believe that, do you?" As usual, he was a little too curious for his own good.

"Why should I doubt his word?"

"He's probably just saying that so we won't be in his way."

"He said to stay here, so we're staying here!"

"All right," Milgic snapped. "I'll go swimming first. You keep a lookout."

"Be careful," Dormiton warned. "That water has a bit of a current."

NICHOLAS T. DAVIS

"I'll be all right," his companion hissed, and jumped into the river. The fury of the river started to carry Milgic away.

"I warned you!" Dormiton yelled, placing the laser in his shoulder holster. He shut the main door hatch and ran after his friend, following the embankment.

After he chased him for almost a mile, he came upon a fallen tree which was in the river. He found the frightened Milgic hanging onto it, gripping tightly. "Stay there!" he yelled, and inched out carefully on the log. Dormiton held his hand out to him, and helped him climb up out of the embankment. "See what I told you! You should start listening before you get us both killed. Let's get back to the ship."

During the lingworts' escapade with the river, Zarcon had reached the waterfall from where Jeff fell earlier. Through his compound eyes he saw the lake and the jungle below. They allowed him to see 360°, like a dragonfly, and enabled him to see many more colors than humans. This also allowed him to detect if he was being followed. He saw the damaged spaceship below, but no sign of Jeff.

He took some rope from his pack to climb down the cliff; tightened it around his waist, and anchored the grappling hook between some rocks. He estimated that the cliff was at least eighty to one hundred feet and was very steep. Below it were several points he could touch down without falling into the river. The water was very turbulent at the bottom, and Zarcon couldn't swim at all. He carefully lowered himself, keeping his clawed feet firmly on the rocks. He used two arms to do the lowering, and two to hold onto the rocks, a task impossible for a human. There wasn't any wind to interfere with the climb, so it went rather smoothly.

When he reached the bottom, he found some rocks to firmly walk on. He jumped to the river edge away from the waterfall. He couldn't see the derelict spacecraft that he saw earlier, but he knew the direction it was in. The lake seemed to span for miles as he gazed out at the water. He knew that something must have happened to his friend because he was nowhere in sight and there weren't any tracks. He didn't want to travel too far, having left the two lingworts alone. He decided to venture towards the wreckage, and hoped it would lead him to his friend. Perhaps Jeff found the vessel and decided to investigate it, but this would not explain why he didn't return. There was a possibility that these lizard creatures either captured or killed him, but he hoped this was not the case. He tied some vines to a tree in an "x" fashion to use as a marker, just in case he got lost.

Proceeding into the jungle, he heard several wild animals. He wasn't scared of them, however, because on his home planet there were much more dangerous creatures stalking the jungles. His friends thought he was a native Belorion, but actually he was from Zacharas, a planet much warmer than this one. On summer days, the surface temperature reached one hundred and thirty degrees, and uninhabitable for a human. In fact, this world was actually quite cool for him.

After traveling another mile, he stopped and dropped his pack to the ground. He opened it, and took out a device about the size of a human palm. This was an electro-metal sensor or EMS for short. It was similar to a metal detector, except for the fact it could also detect electrical impulses up to twenty miles away. He turned it on, and noticed he was getting a faint signal to the north, which was the direction of the wreckage and decided to head in that direction.

He threw his pack back on and kept his laser pistol on his belt within reach, in case he was attacked. He walked in steady strides, using his two top arms to guide his way through the thick vines. The farther he traveled north, the stronger the signal became. He continued to follow the river embankment to keep from getting lost. He realized that his time was growing short, and opened communication with the Rigil Four, using a hand held radio he also brought with him.

"Zarcon to Rigil Four," he said, without an answer. "Zarcon to Rigil Four." After about ten seconds of silence, there was a faint transmission.

"Dormiton speaking," his friend answered. "We had a little trouble learning how to use the radio."

"I'm investigating the wreck of another spaceship out here. I haven't found Jeff yet. How are things there?"

"Okay so far," he answered. "There is no sign of our enemies yet."

"Good," Zarcon said. "Stay there and continue to monitor. I'll be out of your range shortly, so give me some time, maybe about four more hours. If I'm not back by then, you know what to do. The Republic is due here anytime."

"Yes, Sir," the amphibian answered. "Do you think that they have captured him?"

"Not likely. I see nothing to prove that, and I've been traveling a good three miles so far. If I see anything, I'll let you know. Zarcon out."

Zarcon put away his radio and continued towards the craft. The sun was high in the sky by this time and the air became quite muggy, even for a cooler planet such as this one. He stepped on brush that was at least a foot high, which also harbored an alligator that scurried quick into the water when he approached. It startled him, but he wasn't frightened by it. The insect turned, drew his laser to shoot, and put it away after realizing what it was.

The signal on his EMS was rather erratic by the time he reached the wreck. He stepped out into the clearing, inspecting the damage. It wasn't far from the water and if it was indeed a crash, they just missed a softer landing on the lake by a matter of ten feet. He examined the broken hull of the craft and tried to determine its point of origin. He wished there was a way he could tap into the computer of the Rigil Four. At least then he would have a better chance at deciding what it was and where it came from. There were hieroglyphics on it, but he was unable to decipher what they said. He never saw this type before, and it was nothing like the Republic or Tolarion symbols he had seen in the past. They were totally alien to him; he recognized the typical Republic or Tolarion symbols.

He found what was left of the main console; a fragmented piece of metal with melted buttons and a broken viewing screen. Much to his surprise, the distress signal was activated, and still working. There was no way to tell when it was activated, how long it had been going, or what message they left for the rescue party.

There were no bodies present, so he assumed that it crashed a least a year or two prior to their arrival. The metal wasn't rusted, however, indicating that it was from a rather advanced society. They created a metal that wouldn't burn, break, or rust under severe conditions. There were several fresh footprints around the wreckage which belonged to their reptilian visitors and other animals. He decided it was the only clue he had to find Jeff, so he followed them.

It was getting close to noon by the time he reached the halfway point around the lake. The footprints didn't stray far from it, and indicated the creatures stayed close to the water. He only had one hour left before he needed to return, and no way of telling the others of his whereabouts. He realized that finding Jeff this way would take days, but he also knew if he approached by air, they would be in plain view and in even more danger from Riona's men. He needed to help his other friends get out of there before Riona came regardless of what happened to his human friend.

He headed back at running speed, feeling defeated he couldn't help as far as his friend was concerned. "Jeff could be out there,' he thought. 'Dying at the mercy of those creatures, or already captured by Riona or the Tolarions.' He wished there was something else he could do.

By the time he reached the Rigil Four, his friends barricaded themselves behind the main door. It hadn't been opened since the incident on the river. Zarcon entered and dropped his pack and laser. "Did you find him," Dormiton asked.

"No," the insect sighed, who was just as disappointed as they were.

"He's dead," Milgic cried.

"Let's not get worried," Zarcon said. "We have enough to worry about. Riona will be getting here soon, and we need to be ready for him. Milgic, I want you to set up some torches outside in case our reptilian friends come back tonight. Dormiton come with me. We have to find the cobalt we came here for, and set up some traps for Riona and our friends."

The lingworts nodded and followed their orders. Zarcon grabbed a handful of hand held explosives about the size of an orange, and headed out the main door with Dormiton. Milgic followed them and pressed the button to shut the door hatch. The insect placed the bombs in a circular pattern in the jungle surrounding the Rigil Four. The bombs could be triggered by pressure that was applied to them such as a foot stepping on them, or anyone trying to move them after they were activated.

He knew the first thing Riona would do was to try to tap into their thoughts. Zarcon had developed a tolerance for this to some degree, and could block out some of the thought transmissions, but not all of them. Minor things, such as planting explosives could be blocked out by thinking about where his friend might have gone. In their present situation, this could work to their advantage.

By the time the two planted the bombs and found the cobalt, their friend Milgic had set up and lit the torches. They found various berries and fruits to dine on for dinner. It was just before nightfall, and Zarcon told Milgic to keep the first watch. He sat at the open main door, and held his laser gun tight. He was scared, but he knew this instrument of destruction would save him.

As it grew darker, he heard the growling sounds throughout the jungle that became closer. He shouted to Zarcon, who worked on the casing to his jamming device. He jumped up, as Dormiton followed him quickly.

"They're out there!" he stated.

"The light hurts their eyes. As long as those torches are going they won't bother us."

"How can you be so sure?" Milgic asked.

"Because I am," explained Zarcon. "They appear to be afraid of the light. Stay out here with him, Dormiton, I've got to get the casing done. If any of those creatures attack, climb back in the ship and start shooting."

Zarcon went back to finish his task. He melted the cobalt down, shaped it, and formed a crude casing around the wiring in the dimensional tracker device. He was just putting on the finishing touches; and all he needed to do was to test it. That would have to wait, however, until they got off the planet.

The trio found it tough to sleep, as the growling continued through most of the night. Zarcon stayed awake to monitor the scanners and keep watch. It was two days since their arrival and there was still no sign of Riona. He began to wonder if the same thing that happened to Belor happened to Riona as well. Riona seldom let his enemies get the best of him. He fought battles with Balta and the Tolarions for years and never let them get the best of him. They were clever adversaries, even by his standards, and even without his mental power. Balta and Riona were both tyrannical dictators at their best, moving from planet to planet, defying anything that got in their way. The humanoid wasn't any different than a Tolarion; the only difference was Riona used the Republic to do his dirty work.

Zarcon wanted no part in it. He was a being of 'true peace' like his friend Dormiton told him earlier. Unlike his amphibian friend, however, he knew peace would not come without a fight. He summoned the computer for an explanation of what had happened to Belor. The machine responded immediately. "Belor in tact, no life forms indicated," it answered.

"Explain," stated Zarcon.

"Sensors indicate no life readings, other than microscopic life forms."

"Is the planet emitting any radioactivity or electromagnetic impulses?"

"Affirmative, radioactivity is at extremely high level."

Obviously, the base on Belor suffered some kind of attack. The planet was there, all right, but the dome city and force field were destroyed by an explosion, probably from the death ray itself. He hoped the ray gun was destroyed as well, but had a feeling that Riona was somehow behind this. He decided as a last alternative he would find Jeff using the ship's computer.

"Are there any homo sapiens life forms on this planet?" he asked.

"Affirmative. Sensors indicate one homo-sapien life form located three point nine miles from this craft."

"Is it living?"

"Affirmative. Sensors indicate breathing pattern irregular, loss of blood, structural damage in bone in lower right leg, structural damage in bone in left arm."

It was clear to Zarcon Jeff was injured, and possibly dying and hiding. He decided in the morning they would abandon the ship and set out together to find him. If they destroyed the ship at least they could find a place to hide until Riona left. He noticed a faint reading on his scanners coming from beyond their current star system. He guessed that Riona discovered their whereabouts, and was on his way to Zebula. It would take him at least a day to reach them, which gave them little time to find their friend and escape. Zarcon had finished the jamming device in time, and he tried to get some sleep, but it wasn't easy. He lay awake, and thought what to do about Jeff. "I shouldn't have let him go alone,' he thought. Then he thought that wouldn't have mattered anyway, Jeff being as determined as he was. While pondering the situation, he heard scratching at the door. He peered out the viewing screen, and saw the torches had gone out. This led him to believe their visitors knocked them over and were proceeding to claw their way in. He grabbed his laser gun quick as one began to pound on the door. Another beast through his weight into it, and the lingworts awoke. "What are we going to do," yelled Dormiton, as a hand reached in, prying the door open at its crack.

Zarcon fired his laser at the hand, burning it severely. The creature screamed in pain as another hand reached its way through, and began to pry the door again. Zarcon fired again, hitting the creature square in the chest. "Open the main door hatch," he yelled in haste, as the lingworts looked at him as if he was insane. Dormiton tried, but it was jammed.

"It's jammed!" he yelled, as another creature reached in and grabbed Zarcon's leg.

"Help me!" he yelled to his friends, who each grabbed a laser. Dormiton fired, and hit the creature in the arm. The blast of the laser threw him clear across the ship and against the wall. Zarcon stumbled to his feet, as his leg bled from the claws which ripped into him. Another reptile threw his entire body weight against the door, denting it. Zarcon limped to the door, stuck the laser gun through the crack, and fired erratically in all different directions. They heard the screams grow louder and then three minutes later there wasn't a sound.

"Are they gone?" Dormtion asked, as he lifted himself off the floor.

"For the moment," Zarcon said as he examined the damage to the door. "We'll have to stay alert, however. They probably will come back, once they're no longer fearful of us. I can't understand why none of the explosives worked."

"Maybe they found them," Milgic suggested.

"If that's true," Zarcon stated. "They're capable of reason, which I don't believe is the case. Perhaps if we were to offer them food or something they would go away."

"You have got to be kidding!" Milgic laughed. "It's obvious that we're food to them."

"They may have Jeff," Zarcon said. "We've got to find some way to get him back. Are you willing to risk his life for your own?"

"No," Milgic answered. "But we can't make deals with savages, especially if we're their main course!"

"We can't attack them forever either. They'll outnumber us and take the ship anyway," Zarcon said. "Maybe they feel we are a threat and are defending themselves."

"What about defending ourselves?" Dormiton asked.

"I thought you were advocators of peace?" Zarcon joked.

"Not with something as dangerous as they are!" Milgic snapped. "We have to do something!" Zarcon laughed, putting his laser pistol back in his belt around his waist. He was pleased they finally saw his point of view.

"I agree with you. But we have to try at least. If they become violent, then we'll defend ourselves. Agreed," he asked. They nodded, reluctantly.

"I'll go out and try to offer them some of the fish I caught earlier," Zarcon told them. "Leave the main door open, so I can get back in, in case they're hostile."

Zarcon jumped from the ship as they pried the doors open with their hands and a laser rifle. The reptiles were still present, but had backed away from the ship about thirty feet, and didn't even touch the fish hanging on a tree next to the ship. Zarcon could barely endure the pain in his leg as he limped towards them, and raised his arms in the air. "I do not wish to harm you," he said slowly. "We come in peace."

The reptiles' reddish eyes glowed in the darkness as they crept towards him. It was obvious they had seen a spaceship before because they were neither frightened nor bewildered by it. Zarcon couldn't determine whether they could understand him or not, for they didn't answer him

"Have you seen our friend?" he asked. "The human?"

They continued to creep towards him, leading him to believe they had no intention of communicating. He backed up towards the ship and gripped his laser tight. They followed his every movement until he ran towards the door, and several of them attacked him with lightning speed.

Zarcon felt the claws upon him as he fell, dropping his laser to the ground. One grabbed his injured leg and sank its fangs into it, as another bit his top left arm. He found it difficult to escape, even with four arms as the searing pain grew unbearable. Dormiton hit the landing light control which quickly scared them off. He ran out to help their injured friend, with his comrade, Milgic close behind.

"Are you all right?" Milgic yelled, as he bent over Zarcon.

"Not really!" he snapped, trying to block the pain from his mind, finding it

58

extremely difficult.

"What can we do?" Milgic asked.

"There is something," their insect friend gasped. "I must transfer my pain to one of you to heal myself. You'll only be in pain temporarily, and then we both will be okay." He touched Dormiton's head with his gently squeezed right upper claw and began a form of mind transference with the amphibian. Milgic watched as the insect transferred his pain to the lingwort, and his wounds gradually disappeared. Dormiton screamed as he felt every bit of agony his friend went through. When the wounds were gone, the pain subsided as well.

"Are you okay," Milgic asked them both.

"I'm all right," Dormiton answered.

"We'll both be just fine," Zarcon answered, and lifted himself from the sand, feeling drained. "The wounds have disappeared and the pain is gone."

"How?" Milgic questioned.

"By thought transference," he explained. "I used my mind to eliminate the pain. The pain was transferred to Dormiton until I could heal my own wounds. When they healed, there was no longer any pain."

"That's incredible!" Milgic said, as they climbed back in the ship. "Has Riona ever used his power like that?"

"No, as far as I know he never had this ability. Only our kind does." They closed the main door behind them, and then helped Zarcon sit down at the helm.

"You were right," he admitted. "It appears that they do not wish to communicate."

"Do you think they've got Jeff?" Milgic asked.

"Well, they haven't eaten him yet according to the ship's life readings sensors. In the morning we'll get him and get out of here."

"The morning may be too late," Dormiton pleaded.

"We can't attack them at night," Zarcon explained. "They have the advantage. We'll have to wait until morning, and once we find their den or nest, we can attack them by air. According to our sensors, that would be approximately three miles from here."

"Won't we kill Jeff if we do that?" Milgic asked.

"Not if we get him out first. Dormiton will be in charge of that. You and I will need to operate the ship. Right now, we need to get some rest."

"What about those things out there?" Milgic screeched.

"As much as I hate to do it, we'll have to leave the landing lights on," Zarcon said. "I will repair the door first thing in the morning."

Zarcon was uncertain if these creatures slept at all, but he knew bright lights bothered them. If they slept in the daytime, there was at least a chance of saving their friend from impending doom.

The next day, the glare of the black spacecraft was bright as the sun rose above the canyon on Zebula. The inhabitants jumped through the crack of the door and eyed the area for any left over visitors. Dormiton ran to the water to get a drink and felt the current of the water, careful not to make the same mistake his friend Milgic made a day earlier. Milgic followed Dormiton cautiously.

"Enjoy, my friends," Zarcon said, realizing this may be their last swim. He reached inside the craft, pulled out a long, three inch wide plastic tube, and placed it into the water. This was to collect their drinking supply, carried in a tank inside the hull of the ship, which also was part of the shielding system that protected them from gamma rays and radiation. He turned on the pump which circulated the water, and turned towards the damaged door.

Crawling back inside, he searched for a welding device to repair the metal. He noticed the sensors were picking up a number of alien vessels, which were no more than three hours away. He knew that if they wanted to escape, they would have to do it soon-Jeff or no Jeff. "After I'm done with this door, we're getting out of here!" he yelled to his two friends, and jumped back in the ship.

"What about Jeff?" Dormiton asked, running towards him. He knew that neither of them were going to like what he had to say.

"I'm afraid we don't have enough time to save him," he explained. "Riona will be here in less than three hours. We have to get out of here before he gets a link on our minds."

"Can't we escape to the far side of the island?" Milgic asked, as he began to panic.

"He'll find us,' Zarcon answered. "If we remain here, we will die."

"Isn't there anywhere that's safe?" Dormiton asked.

"There is only one place in the universe that's safe," Zarcon stated.

"Where is that?" Milgic asked.

"At the council chambers on Sentros. He cannot harm us there," Zarcon said.

"Why not?" Milgic asked.

"Because his powers are ineffective there. The council is Republic headquarters."

"I thought you said he is the leader of the Republic?" Dormiton questioned.

"He is," Zarcon said, as he repaired the main door. "But he doesn't control them. There are powers in the universe even stronger than his."

"Then I suppose that is our next stop?" Milgic asked, his green eyes fixed on the insect. "After we search for Jeff again, right?"

"No," Zarcon insisted. "We have to distract Riona so he doesn't know we're leaving."

"How?" Milgic asked.

"By creating a small diversion. We'll use that wrecked spaceship as a decoy. I don't want either one of you to think about Jeff. I want you to concentrate on fear, as if we are crashing. Maybe we can trick him into believing we crashed. By the time he gets here, we'll be gone."

"What guarantee do we have that he doesn't already know what we're planning?" Milgic asked in a sarcastic manner.

"He cannot read minds at this range," Zarcon answered.

"That's a relief," Milgic sighed.

"But he will be able to as he reaches orbit, so be prepared," Zarcon commanded.

He finished welding the replacement metal on the door and fixed the circuitry, opened and closed the doors for a test, then ordered them to get on board. After two hours of making sure all systems were running normally, and after putting away the water tubing, they prepared to lift off. The sensors indicated the Republic ships were at the edge of that particular solar system, and they decided to make their move immediately.

Zarcon's scheme would hopefully distract his enemy. They were going to fire the weapons on the area where the spacecraft was, creating an explosion big enough so it would show up on their sensors, and escape just before they landed to investigate. Riona didn't know that Zarcon created a special jamming device, making him invisible to even their scanners.

Zarcon fired the propulsion rockets, which lifted them off the ground, and burned the plants and rocks below them. The lingworts peered out of the viewing screen, the ship slowly rising above the canyon, leaving what they hoped would be a new home. They couldn't help but feel remorse and shame for leaving Jeff behind.

Zarcon also felt this way, but he knew they had to leave, if the rest of their crew were to survive. It was one of the hardest decisions he ever had to make; he just hoped Jeff would stay out of their enemies' hands. Zarcon knew Jeff was the only thing Riona could lock onto and would use him to get to the rest of them. He became more neurotic the more he thought about it. He began to sense the presence of the adversarial tyrant who approached closer to Zebula.

The Rigil Four passed over the lake, and Zarcon instructed the computer to fire the lasers. They struck the clearing where the ship was with pin-point accuracy. 'It seemed a shame to destroy these precious artifacts,' Zarcon thought. The wreckage was obviously from a much superior race than either Belor or Tolaria. He wished for more time to study this strange, mysterious race. He fired the booster rockets, and they headed through the atmosphere towards space.

"Goodbye Jeff Walker," he said, while the lingworts wept. "We'll miss you, my friend." He checked his scanners, making sure Riona was still out of range, and then turned to his two friends.

"I'll need your help," he said. "Dormiton, activate the dimensional transporter and jamming device. We're going to head back to our universe."

The lingwort walked over to the panel. "Which button is it," he asked.

"It should be marked," their commander said. "There is a red button and a green button; press them both." He followed his orders, and the solar flare appeared again and created another wormhole. They traveled through it and found themselves back in their own universe within seconds, and dizzy as ever.

"Plot a course for Sentros, star sector 891101," Zarcon said, as the computer reacted to his command. He then turned to his friends. "We still may have to hijack another ship."

"Why?" Dormiton asked. "We've escaped for the moment. And we've left our best friend there!"

"That moment won't last for long," Zarcon stated. "Riona already has a death warrant out on me, and when he finds out we've escaped him again, he won't be so easy on us!"

"What about Jeff?" Milgic insisted.

"His fate is out of our hands now," Zarcon said.

"He wouldn't leave you here!" Milgic sniped.

"I'm afraid that isn't true," Zarcon replied. "He's courageous, but he's not stupid."

"I still think you're wrong!" Dormiton snapped.

"Look, Guys. I don't like this anymore than you do, but if we did rescue him, we would put all of our lives at risk. Do you want that?" They shook their heads, bowing them. "All right then. Besides, Jeff would have wanted us to finish our mission. Instead of sulking, you should be helping me come up with a plan. We can't just coast into Sentros in an enemy ship unannounced. The Republic will destroy us!"

"What do you suggest we do then?" Milgic asked.

"We send a distress signal," Zarcon replied.

"A distress signal?" Dormiton asked.

"Yes," the scholarly insect stated. "Even if it's a Tolarion ship, they'll investigate it."

"Then what," Milgic asked.

"Then we'll try to explain our situation. The council is bound to help."

"And if they don't," Dormiton questioned.

"Then we won't be any worse off than we already are."

"At least now we're alive and free," Milgic sneered.

"We'll never be free as long as Riona is after us. If the council can't help us, no one can."

Fear and doubt overcame the small crew, as the Tolarion ship traveled through the endless region of space. The doubt of ever reaching home again and fear of what became of their friend plagued their minds. Zarcon couldn't help but feel defeated in the task of rescuing his friends from a certain death. He tried to deal peacefully with his leader, but he knew now that he was beyond reasoning and had slipped towards madness. He also knew he would stop at nothing to seek his revenge against them, even defy the council-if he hadn't already.

CHAPTER SIX

While the lingworts and Zarcon had contemplated the rescue of their friend, a silent force followed them across the vastness of the galaxy. He sat behind his command post, overlooked the screen that lay in front of him, and turned towards a Belorion subordinate at the navigational panel. "How long before we reach Zebula," he asked, in a cold inhuman voice.

"Approximately ten hours, Sir," the Belorion answered.

"Once we reach our destination, I only want two scout ships with me," Riona said. "The rest will remain in a distant orbit to intercept the renegades. I don't want them to escape from me again."

He stared into the empty space of the viewing screen. 'How dare they defy me,' he thought. 'Handful of traitors! At least they will be destroyed here before they can spread their beliefs across the universe!'

As Zebula lay in front of the dark grey Republic ships, even Riona's time was growing short. The Tolarions already blamed the Republic for destroying Zeloria and their ground base on the lingwort's planet, Ventros, and were preparing for an offensive attack. Preparations were being made to send attack ships to Belor and Sentros, the council's home planet.

Riona was not worried; even without an army, his mental powers were a force to be reckoned with. Having the doomsday weapon, as he called it, was just icing on the cake. He felt that no one could stop him, not even this human named 'Jeff Walker.' Even at this distance, he could sense the human was injured, but he couldn't discern any other information yet. Within four or five hours he'd be able to, and then he would have his apostates.

His powers enabled him to read minds as well as control them, move objects with relative ease without touching them, and create illusions to confuse his victims. His only wish was that no one ever discovered his weakness; for if that was to happen, it would spell disaster for him.

Zarcon, unfortunately for him, knew one of them-distraction. Riona knew that his arthropod adversary knew this as well, and was working on a way to overcome this problem. He wanted the meddler dead for some time, but he needed a reason to execute the diplomat, for the Republic wouldn't condone his actions otherwise. Now, with the president of Belor out of his way, he could control the galaxy without interference. There was, however, the matter of the earthling which would be corrected soon.

On the scanners, Riona stared at the bluish-green aquatic world. In a trance, he was only receiving simple thought transmissions from the humanoid. They were thoughts of fear, pain and discomfort. As he probed deeper, he realized the human was surrounded by reptiles of some kind; hideous, blood-thirsty creatures. The darkness he empathized engulfed him like the emptiness of space itself.

As the hours passed, He tried to scan for Zarcon's mind, and found himself unable to. "Prepare to land," he told his second in command. Riona scanned for insect life, but only found traces of smaller specimens. "What game are you up to now, old friend?" Riona stared at the equatorial land masses on the planet below. "We'll need to land at coordinates 9.6501. Near that island below. Confirmation computer?"

"Confirmed," the machine answered. "Coordinates set at 9.6501."

The three hundred and fifty feet craft entered Zebula's atmosphere, withstanding the furious heat against the shields. As the jet-like spaceship glided towards the equator, they switched to sub orbital speed. They approached the canyon on the small island where the Rigil Four was earlier. Riona saw the indentations of where it had landed, and then peered at the clearing where the wreckage was still smoking. "Land near there," he commanded, pointing towards the clearing.

The ship edged into the cloud of smoke that lingered around the lake. The craft landed in the clearing, their commander opened the main hatch, and jumped out onto the soft soil. His subordinates closely followed his orders, and held their weapons firm. "Spread out," he told them, as they immediately dispersed into the jungle. He walked over to some debris that was scattered about, bent over and picked up a piece with unfamiliar writing on it that was definitely not of Tolarion origin. He tried to fuse his mind to the object to determine its origin by holding it in his hand. He performed this type of mind-meld many times before with great success. It would take a little time to do it, and he couldn't be distracted.

He began his trance, as the object took him back to a time when the worlds of Tolaria and Sentros didn't exist. He surmised that the object was a least three billion years old, and questioned how this could even be possible. The metal itself didn't appear that old. He could also approximate its origin, which was somewhere deep within the constellation of Orion in the human's universe. It came from a world extremely technologically advanced; where both space and time were easily traveled, and where peace was the true meaning of life. 'Sentimental fools,' he thought. 'Living for an idea that would never last.' Dwelling further, he saw their planet was destroyed by a supernova, and were forced to leave for a new home. After that, he sensed nothing more about them.

After he realized the explosion was an elaborate hoax, he called for his men to return to the clearing. When they responded, he addressed them, and dropped the object from his hand. "I want the human found!" he roared. "Lieutenant Zaroz?" The lead Belorion in the crew saluted him. Most of his crew was Belorion, but there were other beings as well. "Take five guards and go over to that canyon," Riona told him. "Find him, but don't kill him. I want him alive."

They followed his orders, venturing into the jungle. Riona stared at the debris, smiling. "So you are clever, Zarcon?" he sneered. "How clever will you be when I capture your human friend? You'll feel every bit of the pain I will inflict upon him, and then you'll surrender. And then the Republic will be mine."

While Riona planned his diabolical plot, the human had just awakened from his mishap. Jeff felt the blood that ran from his face, arm, and legs in the darkness of a cavern. He couldn't understand why these creatures didn't harm him. He was only food, like so many other animals they dragged into their lair. They brought him here from the lake, but he was unaware how. It was apparent there wasn't any intention on killing him; they didn't injure him or show hostility towards him at all. When Jeff tried to break a light stick with his good arm, they threw rocks at it to put it out. He groped in the darkness, crawling on the cavern floor. His right leg was broken, and he could only drag himself across the sand. His left arm was broken as well, had a gash about an inch deep, and there was a superficial wound on his head.

He needed to make a tourniquet to stop the bleeding, so he ripped the silky fabric of his spacesuit and tied it tight around his arm with his right hand, using the rest of the cloth to make a sling to reduce the unbearable pain. He could tell it was late afternoon due to the sunlight that came through the entrance of the cavern. Unfortunately, it seemed too high for him to reach in the condition he was in, but decided to at least give it a try.

He dragged his wounded body, as he heard the sounds of the reptiles awaking. They were quick to grab him, and held him as if to suggest him not to leave. "Why are you keeping me here," he painfully asked. There was no answer, only a distinct growling sound, as they held his arms tight, and he screamed in agony.

He knew he couldn't communicate with them, but he had to somehow. He felt for his laser, which for some reason they didn't take away. When they let go of him, he fired in their direction at the ground and they jumped back in fear. He then fired at the rocks with his laser, spelling the word 'peace.' The letters glowed in red, and the reptiles pondered them. They never spoke English before, and they had seen humans before- but from where?

Zeloria was in the other universe, but Earth was in this one. Was it possible they saw humans from Mars or Earth before, or were the Tolarions involved somehow and brought Zelorions here? None of it made any sense to him. They were too primitive to create spaceships of their own, and even if they did, they would also have the problem of inter-dimensional travel, unless they crashed here years ago and regressed evolutionally. According to what Zarcon had told him, there were no intelligent humans within this particular galaxy capable of such travel.

He also wondered how the human from Earth got to Tolaria in the first place to create their tyrannical race. The more he thought about the present, the more he missed the past. He recollected a time when Lori and he were on an expedition on the far side of one of Jupiter's moons, Calissto. The two of them were sent on a scientific mission to collect rock samples from the moon using a planetary drone.

Jeff remembered how beautiful the giant gas planet was as they approached it. He was younger then, about twenty six years old. They gazed at one another, Lori's blond hair flowing to her shoulders, and then at the moon Calissto.

"Pretty isn't it?" she asked him.

"Yes it is," he answered, smiling back into her blue eyes. He didn't want to tell her just yet, but he had strong feelings for her at the time. Space was a very lonely place for him. There were other women at the base, but he always loved Lori, even when they were in the academy together. Other women had nothing in common with him; they were either too pushy or ignored him completely. She was the only one who could ever really understand him.

When the two arrived at Calissto, they sent the probe to collect rock samples and to determine a future base site. Nothing unusual happened on their mission, and after that the two continued to be close friends. They did exchange a brief kiss, but she told him she wasn't ready to make any commitments yet.

Those were the days before she was transferred to base control. He always thought her transfer was a direct result of their involvement with each other, even though his superior, John Carver said it was because of Jeff's inability to follow orders. He would have followed them if he thought they were justified. The transfer ended up being a promotion for her.

Now, ten years later, he longed for any kind of interaction; even the inhabitants that were on Zeloria. It was apparent that their rival, Riona, despite being part human himself, despised humans.

As the glowing rocks faded to a low ember, he saw that his captors didn't understand his message. He dragged himself towards the exit, only to be pushed back down again. Growing impatient, he fired his laser at another one of them, as it jumped in fear. They immediately surrounded him, and he slowly dragged himself across the cavern floor.

They were no longer afraid of the light intensity, and began to adjust to its effects. This was due to the fact they were beginning to live in daylight, and had begun the evolutionary process the computer spoke of. They grabbed the human and carried him into another tunnel which was away from the outside light. He lost his laser when one of them shook it from his hand, so he had no choice at the moment than to do want they wanted him to do.

He felt helpless as he was led to a larger section of the cavern, and sat down on a flat, stone table. The creatures fled the room afterwards, heading in the direction from which they had come, a door shutting the tunnel entrance behind them. The room brightened in an array of colored censored lights, all pointed in Jeff's direction. He eyed the room for some sign of their operator, but saw nothing other than an immense computer, which was too advanced for such a primitive culture.

"Who are you?" he yelled, expecting no answer from the machine.

Much to his surprise, an amplified voice answered. "Welcome," it said. "We are inhabitants of a long dead world called Talok." As the voice spoke, an image appeared on the wall unlike anything he had ever seen. It was that of a being that was half man and half reptile. He was slender and seemed extremely intelligent.

"If you have found this transmission," he continued. "You will know that our world no longer exists, and that my words are true. Many eons ago, a supernova destroyed our planet. We were forced to flee across the universe in hopes of a new beginning, but our people became divided, and began to fight with one another. If you have found this world, you have probably found the survivors, if any, of our race. As I speak, it is most likely evident that an evolutionary process has began on them, as this installation contains the genetic properties to enable them to do so. If you are a human listening to this, there will be no change in your anatomical structure. If you are Talokian, however, you will be altered considerably. You may have traveled here somehow, maybe from a distant star. I wish you luck in your experiences with our race. By the time this transmission is completed, a new race of Talokians will begin. Farewell, Friend, and may peace be with you."

Jeff chuckled at their farewell, knowing there could never be peace in his time. When he sat up on the table, he noticed his bones were no longer broken, and his wounds were completely healed. Feeling a little dazed, he jumped from the table, stumbled briefly, and the tunnel door opened. The Talokian descendants entered, the protégés now appearing much like their mentor on the cavern wall.

"Greetings," the leader said. "My name is Jalok."

"You spoke?" Jeff stated, amazed.

The leader gazed at him, smiling. His eyes were wide open, unlike the blindness they possessed earlier. "Of course I spoke," he said. "We are no longer savages. The genetic process is completed, thanks to you, and we are true Talokians again. We apologize for the way you were treated upon your arrival, it was necessary to get you here. We were primitive creatures of the night when we attacked your ship."

"My ship?" Jeff questioned. "What about it?"

"We attacked it, I'm afraid. Your friends left in it this morning."

"Left?"

"Yes, is there a problem?"

"Something must have gone wrong."

"I don't know. They didn't seem to be scared of us."

"Riona," Jeff surmised. He knew now their enemy was closing in on them. He figured he would be safe as long as he stayed with the Talokians. "There is an alien humanoid chasing us. He wants us for what he calls treason. He is a dictator, and has already destroyed one race of people."

"It sounds as if he has not found peace within his own heart," Jalok said.

"Only then will he realize war is not the way. Our race was virtually eliminated due to such maliciousness towards one another, but we were sent into this galaxy to be reborn."

"How long ago?"

"I cannot say for certain," the reptile said. "As far as we know it was billions of years ago. No record was able to be kept, other than the transmission that you saw and heard, and the knowledge passed onto us by the regenerator through contact with you."

"Why did you need a human?"

"We were once part human, as we are once again."

"Have you ever seen a human here before?"

"No, you are our first. We visited humans millions of years ago, but not on Earth. It is more likely that Earth was populated as a colony from one of those distant planets."

Jeff couldn't believe what he was hearing. Was this really possible? He began to believe anything was possible, having witnessed the improbability of the science he already saw. Even though he was fascinated, he had to get back to the matter at hand.

"Have the Tolarions been here?" he asked.

"What are the Tolarions?" Jalok asked.

"They are ape-like creatures with one eye, and have a nasty reputation for conquest."

"They sound like this Riona that you speak of."

"They are very similar."

"No one has landed here before you." Jeff could tell he was sincere by the way his eyes were fixed upon him.

"Is there any way to contact my friends-a transmitter, mind meld, or something?"

"I'm afraid not," Jalok said. "We just regained the knowledge of our forefathers. It will take some time to rebuild our civilization here, probably about a year of your time."

"Are you serious? That's all it will take you is a year?"

"Yes, we have the technology to complete such a project and more. Your Riona probably destroys a civilization in considerably less time, however."

"Is there any way to get off this planet?"

"No. You are stranded here for the moment just as we are."

"I thought you were capable of building an entire civilization from scratch?"

"We are, but we lack the materials to build you an adequate spacecraft right now. It will take a day or two. We also need you to remain here a day or two to finalize our evolutionary process. After that, you will be free to go."

"I've heard that tune before, but now I feel I can trust you."

"It is the least we can do for you. Why don't you relax in the room you just left, until we can build our hub of the main complex. Perhaps the computer will have answers to questions you may have. Feel free to ask what you like."

"Thank you," Jeff said. "You are the only ones who have agreed to help us."

They directed him back into the large computer room, and he sat down on the stone table. The tunnel door shut, and once again the lights focused on him. He peered at the great wall of machinery.

"I am Varmoth, the Talokian teacher," a voice announced. "Ask me a question, Human."

"Why was I needed to start the Talokian genetic process?"

"You were brought to this chamber because you were needed to activate my memory banks to start the process."

"How is this process possible?"

"I am artificially engineered biological genetic system. I can create biological entities using DNA from various sources or alter those that already exist by blending DNA. I am able to see, hear, feel and think as you do. I was needed to change their structure, just as you were needed to change mine."

"I still don't quite understand, but there are a lot of things I don't understand. How are human genes linked to reptile genes?"

"Many billions of years ago, on Talok we had dinosaurs as you know them. They did not die out, but adapted to their environment. As they grew up along side of humans, there was a merging of the two genes using biogenetics, and the result is what you see now."

"Where am I in relation to my home planet, Mars?"

"Thirteen point five light years away. It would take 70,000 thousand years to reach by your current conventional Martian spacecrafts, and a few hundred using your current mode of travel."

"Is there any way of reaching it sooner?"

"Yes, but you are not in access of such a device."

"Could the Talokians build such a device?"

"Yes, but it would take at least two months, even by our standards."

"Is there any other way?"

"Only through time travel or inter-dimensional travel."

"How could I have gotten to another region of space without my knowledge?"

"I cannot answer that. Possibly through inter-dimensional travel."

"That would explain a lot of things," Jeff replied. "Do you think that I was brought to another universe somehow?"

"Affirmative."

"Explain the inter-dimensional process to me."

"Dimensional transporting is a process in which a device converts exotic matter, dark energy or antimatter into energy by using the density of a star, binary star or a black hole. This energy created forms what you call a wormhole or singularity. The wormhole generating device allows an opening of space and time, permitting one to either go forward in time, travel to a parallel universe, or to

69

another location within the same universe."

"Could you explain what happened to the Talokians, and why they were able to survive so long?"

"The Talokians were a highly advanced race from Talok, a planet deep within the constellation of Orion. They existed long before your planet Mars was formed, and traveled the universe seeking others who were as peaceful as they were. They achieved a universal understanding, and invented several serums to diseases that may have killed your people in the past. About three billion years ago, their sun exploded, and destroyed their world. Those who managed to escape traveled throughout the universe in search of a new home. Their peace did not last, as they became corrupted on their journey, and fought with each other. Those who survived knew they had to preserve what knowledge they possessed for future civilizations. That is why they came here. They built this complex which has survived the bonds of time itself."

"How old is this place?"

"2.4334 billion years old."

"How is that possible?"

"This world knows no time. It has remained the same since the Talokians' arrival."

"Nothing can stay the same for that long a time. Every world must change somehow."

"Not this one."

"What about when your sun dies?"

"Then, and only then, will we parish as well."

"Wouldn't the atmosphere have deteriorated long ago?"

"I provide the atmosphere, as I provide the vegetation, the water, and the mountains."

"You can control a planet?"

"Yes. I provide the life sustaining properties, and the world itself does the rest. Without me, it would eventually die."

Jeff contemplated a plan. "Can you create an ion storm?" he asked, knowing it would cause Riona's ship to be disabled. He then would have enough time to destroy his ship and end his evil plan here.

"Of course," the computer replied, as its panel lit up erratically, and within moments, it completed the task. "Ion storm will start in approximately three hours. The main hub of the complex must be completed first."

The storm would last several hours and totally disable their spacecraft for days, enabling the Talokians enough time to complete their task and for them to construct a ship so Jeff could escape. Since Riona had already landed, time was of the essence. Even if Jeff destroyed his ship, he'd still have to deal with the humanoid, and find a way to kill him.

The tunnel door opened hours later, and revealed the complex they had constructed in the canyon cavern. Jeff left the canyon cavern, marveling the structure, as he walked across a constructed wooden suspension bridge towards the object, which was over the waterfall. By now he was sure that Riona saw it as well, but maybe not since the storm had begun, and the visibility was deteriorating. The only other place he saw structures like these were on Belor, and once again he felt primitive and inferior compared to them. How could such a superior race possibly need his help?

The complex was immense, perhaps the size of modern day aircraft carrier. They built it within the gigantic ravine; taking advantage of its elusiveness, and it was only visible from above the canyon and from the south end of the lake. It was made of marble and stone, and indestructible to the elements. Jeff was bewildered at how they made such an advanced structure in three hours. It apparently used some form of power to run it, but what? Its shape was spherical, which made it even more perplexing, and there were no windows, and only one entrance he could see, which was at the end of the bridge he was on. It had writing on it next to the door, and a hand print drawing, which was most likely their own genetic code of entering.

The storm affected the atmosphere, and caused high winds and lightning. He knew Riona would be looking for him, and he needed to find shelter. He placed his hand on the drawing, and the complex door opened, and revealed a large long corridor. Jeff entered as he looked behind him to make sure he wasn't followed.

When the human entered, he saw the tunnel was extremely well lit and quiet. He was amazed at the fact that just a handful of beings could construct such a massive complex in just a matter of hours. It wasn't possible by the laws of the universe or physics. Then again, the more he thought about everything he had seen up to this point was against the laws of physics.

At the end of the corridor, he was greeted by Jalok and a couple of his subordinates. "Ah, Human," he said. "We were expecting that you would return."

"Call me Jeff. My name is Jeff Walker." Jeff scratched his dirty, unkempt hair and beard.

"Of course, Mr. Walker. We have been working on your ship, but we still cannot find some of the essential elements needed to build it within this vicinity."

"That's okay," Jeff said. "I feel safer here than outside right now, even if I am stranded. Is there anything that I can eat, a place to rest, maybe a shower or a bath?"

"You will find everything that you need within your quarters," Jalok said. "Barva will show you the way." He placed his hand on the shoulder of his companion to the right.

Jeff followed the large reptile-human hybrid down several corridors until they came to various chambers on both sides of the hall. They all contained the same handprints he saw on the main entrance.

"This will be your quarters," he said, as he placed his hand on the design. The door opened, and revealed an enormous room with very elegant furniture.

"We've done some research on your culture. I'm sure you will find it to your liking."

He did indeed find it to his liking as he felt the soft blue fabric of the sofa, and the softness of the silk sheets on the bed. He didn't have anything so comfortable since he was back on Mars. As he eyed the bathroom, it felt good to also finally be able to have a good hot shower and shave. The Talokian followed him as he walked to the kitchen area, which even had fruit and some vegetables for him to snack on. There was a little cooked fish with some rice on the table as well. "There is a small bar over there if you become thirsty," Barva said. "I'm afraid we only have our type of alcoholic beverages, however."

He pressed a button on the wall, which opened a door to a compartment. Behind it were various colored beverages. He decided to go with the red fluid, and poured himself a drink. He tasted the sweet beverage which had a slight kick to it, as he coughed. "Not bad," Jeff said in approval. "You don't know how long it's been since I had any of this stuff."

"Do you wish for something to read, or watch on our viewing screen?" Barva asked.

"Do you receive signals from other worlds?" the human asked, as he wiped his mouth on his sleeve. Jeff was surprised they actually had such a concept.

"We don't," Barva explained. "Everything that you see on the screen is artifacts of your past and present, manufactured to your liking."

"From your Talokian teacher, no doubt."

"Exactly. It knows every thought you possess, even the unpleasant ones. Is there anything you would like to recollect on? The computer can take you back to experience your own past."

"Yes, come to think of it, there are some memories I would like to relive."

"Place your hand on the panel," Barva said, and directed him to the wall panel. Jeff placed his hand on the print of it, and another door opened, which revealed a twenty feet wide by twenty feet high screen.

"Now place this upon your head." He handed him a brass ring which fit snug around his head. He pressed a button marked 'mind probe,' and the human began to see images on the screen of exactly what he was thinking.

"Now," Barva said. "Relax your mind, thinking of only the thoughts that you want to."

He saw his close friend Lori on the screen. Her curly, golden hair glistened in the sunlight of the Martian artificial forest. She smiled at him, and laughed at a joke he told. They were on a small picnic, and he just opened a bottle of champagne he brought with them. They were celebrating her promotion to the main control center, and they toasted their glasses together.

"To best friends," Jeff smiled.

"To best friends," she answered, sipping her champagne.

"Does this mean I have to call you Maam now?"

"Only if you want to. Just call me Commander when we're around brass. At least when we're alone you don't have to be totally formal."

"Only half formal. Commander it is," Jeff said, as he peered at the man-made lake that was just twenty feet away. "Would you like to go for a swim?"

"Sure," she answered, as the two walked towards the water. As the human saw a slice of his past, he missed home again. The screen changed as quickly as his mind and he saw images of his childhood, about the time he was five.

"Dad?" Jeff asked his father. "How long does it take to get to take to get to Earth?" His father put his hand on his shoulder.

"Why do you want to know that?" he asked him.

"I was just wondering, that's all," Jeff said. "I want to be a flight commander someday- just like you."

"A long time, Son. About four months."

"Do you sleep on the way?"

"Part of the time, yes."

Reliving his childhood at eight years old, he remembered his parents' accident as well. He was surprised the mind probe enabled him to see other people's past as clear as his own. Even though he was with his Uncle Clark at the time, he saw what happened to them during their flight. They were onboard an interstellar spacecraft which was sent to the Earth's space station Edronomis for a three hundred passenger pickup to return to Mars. The warning light came on and one of the fuel tanks exploded. The craft lost altitude, and plummeted through the atmosphere towards the ocean helplessly. Jeff could hear, see, and feel their fear and agony as he placed his arms against the screen. His mother grabbed his father's arm, and buried her head against his shoulder in fear. They both cried, until the crash broke Jeff's concentration from the mind probe. He violently threw the headband to the floor is disgust. Sweat poured from his body, as he fell to the floor and wept. Barva placed his hand upon the man's shoulder, trying to console him.

"Take care, Friend," he said. "You must learn to accept what is, and concentrate on your inner happiness. Otherwise your future will be as grim as your past."

"But I should have been there with them?" he cried.

"You couldn't have been," the reptilian creature said. "You were just a child. You had no way of knowing that would happen, just as you had no way of knowing that Balta would attack Lingwort."

"How do you know about that?" Jeff asked. "Can you read minds too?"

"In a sense. The teacher teaches us everything it knows, and it senses your thoughts as if they were our own. We are connected through the teacher as it is connected through you."

"That is definitely one awesome computer," Jeff stated. "Your people have saved my life. I wish there was something I could do for you."

"If it wasn't for us, your life probably wouldn't have been in danger. There is one thing you can do. Continue to spread our word of peace throughout your travels."

"That might be a little difficult, even if I do escape here. You see I'm dealing with two tyrannical societies and we're kind of right in the middle of their war with each other."

"Then, as unfortunate as it may sound, you have to somehow diffuse the two societies' conflict. You have our support."

"I thought you were peaceful?"

"Peaceful, yes, but not vulnerable. We realize that force is sometimes necessary to maintain peace within the universes."

"That's what I've been trying to tell my friends," Jeff explained. "They believe in absolute peace to the point of refusing to protect themselves!"

"They are a primitive race, however, and you cannot expect them to understand. They have found peace within themselves and their brothers. They haven't even really learned what good and evil is yet."

"Are you saying that I made a mistake by bringing them?"

"Varmoth believes so, but I personally do not. You saved them from an almost certain death. There is no guarantee that the rest of their race will remain unchanged. The Tolarions, as you call them, will probably return to destroy them." Jeff believed they were truthful and compassionate beings, despite their frightening appearance.

"Is there any way of stopping them?"

"Yes, if it's not too late."

"I really could use your help. I'm afraid I don't know where my friends have gone."

"We will be glad to assist you in any way we can."

"Thank you. I'm a little tired still, do you mind if I rest for a while?"

"No, not at all. Your ship will be ready in a day or two as promised. A small fleet of our own ships will accompany you in about four weeks."

"Can you really build them that fast?"

"Yes," Barva explained. "They will all be built simultaneously. We'll need the location of the Tolarion planet, and the other nemesis that plagues you."

"I'm afraid I won't be much help in that department," Jeff stated. "Zarcon is from the Republic, and has that information as well as the ship's computer banks."

"We'll have to find him then. Where do you think he might have gone?"

"He did mention something about a council, but I don't know where their headquarters are. "I'll try my best," Jeff replied. "At least now I don't feel totally alone."

"You're never alone," the Talokian philosophized. "If you find peace within yourself and within your heart."

He left the human staring at the empty mind probe screen. He realized even without human companionship, there was perhaps some truth to that prospect-maybe he wasn't as alone as he thought after all.

CHAPTER SEVEN

Riona and his men returned to their ship to find out the storm had temporarily disabled the computer systems. Lieutenant Zaroz accompanied him as they entered the craft. Riona sat down at his command chair, disgusted, and defeated. "Where is that human?" he snapped. "I can't even register his thought patterns!"

"Perhaps he escaped with Zarcon?" Zaroz suggested.

"Impossible," Riona sneered. "I could sense him when we landed."

"Perhaps you are wrong?"

"Wrong!" Riona yelled. "I'm never wrong about my powers."

"Sorry, Sir," Zaroz answered in a solemn tone, knowing how determined he could be.

"No, he's still here," the humanoid hissed. "But something is blocking my abilities, perhaps it's the storm. Did you get any readings of intelligent life here, Sergeant?"

"No Sir," the sergeant, who was also a Belorion, answered. "The sensors indicated only insignificant plant and animal life before they went out."

"Could an intelligent life form be causing this negative interference?" Riona asked.

"It's possible," their chief science officer said, a human with black hair, a rather wiry build and five feet tall. "But it would need a tremendous amount of energy to do so. Almost as much as a wormhole generator."

"Lieutenant, I want you to find a way of getting the engines back on. Sergeant, bring some men and come with me. We're going to investigate this. We'll head towards the caverns we spotted."

The tidal surge of the approaching storm began to engulf the island's beaches. They ventured as quickly as possible in the direction Riona had sensed the human earlier. It was only a matter of hours before the low land would be underwater, and their spaceship would sink in the mud. Riona told them he wanted the doomsday weapon, which was being stored in the ship's cargo bay, to be saved at any cost, even their own lives. While the storm ripped apart sections of trees that lay in front of them, his men began to panic.

"Relax," he told them. "It's just a storm! Stay in formation!"

He started to wonder if Walker evaded him somehow; perhaps leaving the planet before the storm. That seemed unlikely to the humanoid because his controls would be affected the same way any other ship would, unless they worked on some other technology he was unaware of. He knew the ship they stole was Tolarion, and more primitive than his, and the storm was too powerful for a ship to maneuver in. Sure this human was an excellent pilot and extremely clever, but he couldn't escape without help; the orbiting ships would still detect them and do something to stop him. Their photon laser banks were inoperative, but the Republic's ships also possessed photon missiles that worked on a manual jettison device.

They came upon the huge complex that lay in the canyon over the waterfall. After two hours of fighting their way through the thickness of the wet jungle and driving winds, Riona and his men climbed their way up to where the bridge was, and came upon the entrance which was completely sealed. He turned towards the science officer, and grabbed him tight around the collar in angst. "No intelligent life, Huh?"

"Maybe the sensors went haywire before the storm," the science officer said over the howling winds.

"Yes," Riona said as he let him go. "That must be it! Let's see if we can get in!"

The rain pounded against their faces, and the science officer placed his hand upon the insignia on the door. It would not open for him. "There must be a code," suggested the sergeant.

"I'll show it my code!" Riona yelled, as he drew his laser and fired. The door still remained intact. "It must be some kind of metal alloy that resists heat! Let's take cover in the cavern over there!"

The troop of twenty men ran to the cavern at the end of the bridge to seek shelter from the tropical storm. Several hours passed since the departure of the Talokians and the only thing that remained in them was their complex teacher, Varmoth. When the troop entered the cavern, the door to his chamber sealed shut.

"What was that noise?" the sergeant asked. Riona turned on a light on the front of his suit, similar to a flashlight. He pointed in the direction of the sealed tunnel.

"It appears to be a tunnel of some kind," he stated. "Perhaps the human hides there! Let's find out, shall we?" He pulled an explosive from his pack, and the other men scrambled in haste. He threw it at the entrance, making no effort to do the same. The entrance violently exploded, and sent rocks and debris on him which he shielded by his arm, but remained unscathed. Laughing wildly, he watched his men scurry to the entrance of the cave. The tunnel door was destroyed, and the master computer revealed itself.

"What are you waiting for?" he asked his frightened men. "An invitation?" His men reluctantly followed him as he entered. Riona gazed at the complex machinery in disbelief. "What a fascinating machine. "An inferior life form, my eye."

"Who has desecrated my chambers?" Varmoth questioned, his face appearing on the wall. Riona searched the room to see where the voice came from.

"It is I," he answered. "Riona, leader of the Galactic Republic of Peaceful Civilizations!"

"I have no records in my memory banks of such a person. Please wait, while

I check them again."

"What is causing this storm?" Riona asked the device.

"I am unable to determine that at this time. Please wait, while I check your identification for authorization."

The humanoid grew impatient, wanted answers and didn't care how he got them. He drew his laser and pointed at the computer. "Tell me what I want to know or I'll destroy your memory banks!" he shouted.

"Do you think that is wise?" the sergeant asked.

"It's just a computer left over from an ancient civilization," Riona barked. "It's of no use to us."

"No hostilities will be tolerated," Varmoth said, building a reddish force field around itself.

"What can it do to me?" Riona jested, and fired his laser pistol which didn't penetrate the force field. "So you have your own defense, Heh? Most ingenious."

"What do you want?" Varmoth asked.

"I am looking for a human named Jeff Walker. Perhaps you've heard of him?"

"There has never been a human here. We are a reptilian race."

"For a computer, you lie exceptionally well," the commander hissed. "Would you like to try again?"

"You are intruders, and must be dealt with accordingly," Varmoth stated. "You do not bring peace, only destruction. You must be terminated."

"No my friend," Riona said, realizing he was getting nowhere. He pulled three explosives from his waist, and set their timers. "You must be terminated." His men scrambled from the cavern onto the bridge in fear, as he dropped the explosives and casually left himself.

They ran out and the hillside exploded, sending debris down the canyon. Boulders fell on the Talokian structure, but didn't damage it one bit. Riona laughed wildly, watching the cavern caved in. He believed he achieved a great accomplishment, but in reality, he achieved nothing. The Talokians no longer needed their teacher to survive, only Jeff to merge with the new computer in the complex one more time.

Meanwhile inside the complex, Jeff awoke from his undisturbed sleep, and was greeted by Jalok. He slept through until the next morning.

"I hope that you had a good night's sleep," he said. "It appears that your foe has stumbled onto us. He has just destroyed Varmoth."

"Aren't you in danger now?" Jeff asked.

"On the contrary," Jalok stated. "The teacher has served its purpose, and after tomorrow, you will have served yours here. There is no way they can get in this complex."

"You don't know him very well," Jeff laughed. "He may use his death ray on this planet."

"His death ray is inoperative at the moment, and even if it wasn't, he cannot penetrate our planetary force field. We have exactly two hours before the storm subsides. It will take him at least a day to repair his ship. By then, you'll be safely off the planet."

"I hope you're right," Jeff sighed. "Is my ship ready yet?"

"It will be, and we will assist you with your efforts. Barva and a small crew will escort you to the council of the Republic."

"I told Barva I don't know where it is," Jeff said. "Even if I did, you can't get there without entering the other universe."

"We have read your nemesis' mind to extract the information that you seek. He is determined to stop you, but once again he will fail. The Galactic Republic no longer trusts him, for he has broken several of their treaties already."

"Is that where Zarcon is heading?"

"I don't know, but I would surmise that is the case."

"What about this place?"

"I will remain here as leader of our race with some of our people. The rest will travel later to join you in battle."

"Is that wise? There aren't many of you to begin with."

"We are a prolific surviving race," Jalok said. "Only a handful of us are needed to rejuvenate the species. Riona is of no threat to us. We have telepathic abilities of our own, and he cannot harm us."

Jeff wondered if Riona wasn't somehow distantly linked to this race. It wouldn't seem impossible, being ancestors of some hybrid race, their survivors disbanded across the universe. The tyrant never did disclose his point of origin, and he was unlike any being he came across in the past. He also wondered if the human in the Tolarion records was indeed Riona and was involved in an accident, or some kind of transformation.

"Come let me show you to your new craft," Jalok said, as Jeff rose from the bed. "You'll find it much more advanced then your old one."

"Does it have one of those fancy dimensional transporters?" Jeff asked.

"I'm afraid not," Jalok said, as he directed Jeff down the hallway. "You will have to disable one of Riona's ships, board it, and steal the device onboard. Barva knows how to do this. You will then be able to cross over into the other universe. Our fleet will have to do the same as we don't have the technology to make the devices soon enough. Perhaps when the Tolarions ships come, we will be able to disable some of them as well."

They entered a gigantic room that was in the center of the complex, which contained several spaceships being built. They were shaped like the Tolarions' only flatter and more aerodynamic. They were silver colored, about one hundred and seventy feet in length, and very similar to the flying saucers that were spoken of in the old days when space travel was in its infancy. Jeff could only guess what propulsion system was in them; he felt awed and amazed at how far they came in just one day. Perhaps the Republic and the Tolarions had a lot to learn from these survivors of a lost race.

As he approached one of the ships, Jalok placed his hand upon his shoulder. "Tomorrow will be a new era," he lectured. "An era of benevolence; an era where civilizations can cooperate towards a common goal. We will need you one more time to merge with the new computer in this complex. It will take about two of your hours to complete; you can rest for the remainder of the day and tonight, and leave in the morning."

"What about Riona?"

"We will deal with him in our own way."

"If he fixes his weapon before tomorrow, he will destroy you."

"Then we must make sure he doesn't repair it before tomorrow. We better get you to the transformation chamber. The storm is beginning to subside, and Riona's men are working on their controls. You don't have much time."

He was shown the way to the chamber and the process of transferring a copy of the man's DNA into the complex's memory banks began. After the best night of sleep he had in years, he followed Barva and Jalok down to the hangar bay. They approached his craft, Barva boarded, and Jalok addressed Jeff.

"Barva will instruct you on how the vessel works, and any other questions you might have," he said. "Good luck, Mr. Walker."

"Thanks," Jeff answered as he shook his hand. "I'm going to need it."

He nodded, and Jalok helped him into the craft. He was greeted by Barva, who was sitting in a large chair at the helm. "Hello, again, Mr. Walker."

He nodded, grabbed a helmet and placed it on his head. "How does this ship work?" he asked.

"It's telepathically operated. It responds much in the same way Varmoth does, to the stimuli around it. You command it with your mind."

"Isn't that risky? What if something goes wrong?"

"If anything does, you will press this." He pointed to a blue button on the console. "It will transfer the ship to the computer's control, handling life support systems, plasma based weapons defense and offense, and navigational control."

"What if the ship is about to be attacked by a fleet of ships?"

"It has a self destruct sequence, just as yours did. You have exactly three minutes to evacuate the ship using the ejection chamber."

"And you say this ship is fast?"

"We'll be able to reach the council in three days, which is only a third of the time of your Rigil Four, once we can cross over to the other universe."

"Well, we better get started then. How many ships are going to meet us at the rendezvous point?"

"We'll have a fleet of twenty ships in about four weeks. It will take your enemy awhile to find us."

"I hope you're right," Jeff answered. "I'm counting on that time to escape."

They prepared for liftoff, and the ceiling of the gigantic room opened, as the spaceship slowly began to rise. Riona, who was outside all night trying to find a way in, watched in disbelief as the ship exited the structure.

"Blast that human!" he cursed, as his thought transmissions locked onto him. "He's going to the council! Back to the ship!" He watched the sky, which was now clearer, but still raining lightly. He ran quickly through the jungle, his men followed, and watched the ship ascend into the sky.

"Lieutenant Zaroz, come in," he said into his communication device.

"Lieutenant Zaroz here," his subordinate answered.

"The human is escaping!" Riona yelled. "Notify the fleet immediately! Don't let them pass!"

The Talokian ship entered the atmosphere, and it was apparently clear that Riona was no match for this new technology. Barva placed a tractor beam on one of the drifting Republic ships, and approached it to dock. When it docked, Barva left the helm, and another Talokian took over. "Stay here," he told Jeff. "We are professionals at this. We will be back in ten minutes."

Barva left the craft with two of the ten men crew and entered the drifting craft. A human onboard tried to fire his laser, but when Jalok waved his arm, the gun fell to the floor. He then touched him on the forehead and caused him to fall asleep. Two more men attacked, and the two other Talokians mimicked his actions. When the rest of the crew attacked, the Talokians picked up the lasers and fired at them, wounding them, but not killing them. They went to work on dismantling the dimensional transporter device, and brought it back to the other ship within minutes.

"Get us out of here, Navigator," Barva told the helmsman as they reentered the Talokian craft.

The ship then flew by the fleet so quick that they barely registered on their scanners, which just became active again. This infuriated Riona, who just got back to his own ship, which was beginning to sink in the mud. "They've escaped, Sir," Zaroz reported.

"What do you mean they've escaped?" Riona yelled, pushing his Lieutenant against the wall. "You were supposed to tell the fleet!"

"I did," he answered. "The fleet did not detect them until it was too late. They have a spaceship faster than we've ever seen."

"Indeed," Riona envied, as he released the insect.

"There's something else, Sir."

"Yes?"

"They've hijacked one of our ships and stole the dimensional transporter device."

"They are an advanced race, and at the moment it appears they're assisting our human friend," Riona said, a little more calm now. "Well that's just fine. When we get the ship to maximum range, we'll activate the fusion ray and destroy this puny little planet, and maybe then he'll surrender."

"Sir, surely you don't mean that?" the Belorion Sergeant pleaded.

"You're damn right I do! Do you think I care about some ancient alien race? I'm more concerned about finding the renegades and ending this once and for all!"

His men began to question his sanity. This whole fiasco had become his own personal vendetta against the human and Zarcon, and placed all their lives in jeopardy. He no longer cared about peace or the republic, and although they knew he had always been demanding, they never knew him to become obsessed with power beyond reason. Nonetheless, most of them would never question his orders, for fear they would be executed. Riona had several conflicts in the past with Zarcon the Belorion, but it was never any more than an exchange of violent words. They resolved their disputes in a civilized manner in past discussions. All the crew knew of the incident on Belor was that Zarcon was wanted for treason and was to be captured at any costs. They didn't know those were Riona's orders, not the Republic's.

Their leader began to reassemble his damaged fleet of ships, and realized at one point he would have to go on alone. If word got back that he disobeyed orders, he would lose command, and would no longer be trusted. He was powerful, but not enough to defeat the whole crew. He still had the 'planet destroyer', however, and as long as this was the case, there was nothing in either universe that could stop him.

The long, menacing weapon's nozzle pointed out of its new resting place towards the earth-like world. Its sinister owner peered at the main viewing screen, contemplating whether or not to attack. He decided not to hesitate, and pressed the firing button. The ray didn't hit the surface upon firing; there was a force field around the planet. "Curses," he hissed. "It appears I've underestimated these aliens. Any sign of the human's ship, Lieutenant?"

"No Sir," the Belorion answered. "They're completely out of range."

"Very well. Set a course for Sentros."

"Yes, Sir," Zaroz said, and instructed the computer to command navigational controls, prepare for wormhole generation, and lock in the proper coordinates.

"We'll find the human and Zarcon first," Riona snarled. "Then we'll destroy this insignificant world!"

"Why don't you just leave them be?" Zaroz asked. "They've done nothing to you."

"Nothing yet," suggested Riona. "They did allow the renegades to escape, however."

"Your renegades!" Zaroz boldly defied him. "The federation only seeks Zarcon for questioning concerning the Zelorion incident. The others have done nothing!"

"Silence!" the humanoid roared. "Are you forgetting who the superior officer is?"

"Not anymore," Zaroz said. "I've checked with Dr. Valoria, and he is in full agreement with me. You are suffering from some kind of mental illness that has driven you mad. You are to be relieved of command." The doctor nodded, who was an alien with reddish brown skin and humanoid, with bumps on his forehead, blue eyes and rather large ears.

"Relieved of command," the tyrant laughed. "You must be joking?"

"No, Sir," Zaroz answered. "We have notified the Republic of your behavior. You are to be relieved of command, and placed into custody until we reach Sentros."

"The federation is giving me orders? I am the president of the council!"

"It appears that you longer are. They will no longer succumb to your threats."

"The only threats around here are those renegades! They're the cause of this!"

"They didn't start this, Sir, you did."

"You think you're clever, don't you? How clever will you be if I left you to die on some lifeless world? If you want my command, Lieutenant, why don't you take it from me?"

"Please do not force me to make that decision."

"You can't force me to give up command," Riona reasoned. "You have no special powers to defeat me."

"I do have orders from the council," he said, pulling out his laser. "You as a Galactic Republic officer should respect those orders. And as you know as an officer, I am confident in following those orders through."

"Perhaps you might reconsider?" Riona suggested.

"I don't think so." Zaroz held his laser firm even though he was completely terrified of him.

"Very well," his commander said, as his subordinate lost control of his right lower claw, and pointed the weapon back towards himself. He tried to fight it, but couldn't, and found himself slowing pulling the trigger with his left lower claw. Riona laughed as his men watched in disbelief, and the laser burned through the Belorion's chest, and left him dead on the floor. Riona turned to his terrified crew who grew intensely quiet. "Are there any more defectors?"

It remained quiet, as he read each and every one of their minds, and sensed their fear. "Very well," he said. "You will no longer question my orders. If you do, I will kill you. If you don't follow them, I will kill you. If you think about any type of escape, or notify the Republic, you will be killed. Sergeant, activate all tracking systems. I want the renegades found!"

Riona checked the scanners and the reluctant Belorion followed his orders. The humanoid lifted his head, addressing the computer. "Lock the fusion weapon on all ships in the vicinity except this one."

"Sir," the sergeant pleaded. "You can't do this!"

"Silence!" growled the tyrant. "Unless you want to join your fellow Belorion." They were all stunned at his behavior, and realized the lieutenant was right about his sanity.

"Awaiting fusion ray sequence," the computer answered.

"Sequence 89786756.3., Commander Riona speaking.

"Sequence initiated," the computer answered. "Will begin countdown on

82

your order."

"Begin countdown. Activate engines to full power."

The computer began its countdown, and the lone Republic ship ventured into the darkness. While his men watched the viewing screen, the fleet disappeared from their range. All that remained after the explosions was a brightness, which looked like a small exploding star as the fleet was incinerated and faded into the blackness. They didn't know where the tyrant was taking them, or what his sinister plot was. They just knew Riona savagely murdered their lieutenant and fellow soldiers. An officer they once admired had lost his mind, and with the doomsday weapon, it made him all the more dangerous.

CHAPTER EIGHT

The Rigil Four floated silently through space, and its crew remained just as quiet. There wasn't much to be said; it just wasn't the same without Jeff. Even Milgic, who was usually quite talkative, was at a loss for words.

They were three days away from their arrival to Sentros, and had activated the distress signal. They just entered into the Republic's range and were waiting for a scout ship to find them. Zarcon decided it would be imprudent to use the ship's name or his own name until they were within visual range. The Republic would see it as a threat and attack.

He wondered if Jeff was even still alive. He knew the human was badly hurt, and left with the reptiles, but nothing else. If Riona captured him, he probably wouldn't kill him right away because he needed him, just as he needed Zarcon for his complex game of control. He didn't know why the Republic would go along with his plan; it just didn't seem logical to him.

As they approached Sentros, Zarcon recollected a time when matters were much simpler. There was a time when the Tolarions were allies of the federation, and assisted them in forming all kinds of governments on far away planets. Although both societies relied heavily upon their military's strength, they were partners with one another. After that, both governments began to deteriorate. They began raiding each other's colonies, and building stronger weapons to use against one another. Riona, who was already in power at the time, was more of a diplomat than a dictator. His mental power had somehow corrupted his judgment. Zarcon warned the council of his recent behavior, but they dismissed it as being overzealous about the Tolarion threat.

They would soon realize his maniacal tendencies caused him to break several peace treaties. They could no longer look the other way on this, for it meant fighting a war of unseen devastation. The Tolarions were a militant society, but they used to believe in some peaceful virtues; the worlds who considered trade with them or information they could use were the worlds they respected treaties with, and Republic outposts were usually off limits to them, unless hostility was provoked.

Riona had done just that. Zeloria was an insignificant world in the Tolarion star system, but it was one of their greatest allies. Now they would probably launch a full scale invasion on Sentros unless the council sent a fleet of their own to intercept them.

It was obvious peace couldn't be reached by making treaties. The leader of the council was absent for negotiations, and there was no guarantee he was sane enough to do so anyways. Balar, a humanoid from Befa Seven was second in command, and had just made preparations to embark to Alokia for negotiations. He knew this required great care; their enemies were becoming too aggressive for negotiations and they already received news of reported attacks on some of the smaller populations of the Galactic Republic's territories.

Zarcon and his friends experienced a feeling of doom over them, and knew they were right in the middle of the conflict. Even if the Republic received their distress call, there was no guarantee they wouldn't attack them before they were able to make contact. With that thought in mind, he switched the engines to sub interstellar speed and opened communications.

"Sentros, come in," he said. "Please come in, Sentros."

There was no answer. "We must be out of range," Zarcon said to his two companions. "We'll try again later."

Just as he was about to close communications, there was a faint transmission. "Walker here," it said, as Zarcon glanced at the open space in front of him. He couldn't believe what he was hearing. Was it really Jeff?" The lingworts' green eyes grew wide in glee.

"That sounded like Jeff!" Dormiton yelled, as he ran to the helm.

"Walker here," he said again. "Please respond."

"Jeff," Zarcon answered. "Is that you?"

"Yep," he answered. "I'm right on your tail. At present speed, we should rendezvous with you in six hours."

"But how?" Zarcon questioned. "How could you be alive?"

"It's a long story. When I have time, I'll explain it to you."

"You said 'we.' Who is with you?" Zarcon asked.

"A race called the Talokians. They are the reptilian creatures that we came across," Jeff explained. "They've seemed to have undergone some kind of evolutionary process. I still don't quite understand it myself. They've agreed to help us."

"What is he talking about?" Milgic asked.

"It appears that our reptile friends were more than they appeared to be," Zarcon stated, as he recollected the derelict spaceship. "Jeff, was that damaged spaceship we found theirs?"

"In a sense," Jeff answered. "It belonged to their ancestors."

"Any sign of Riona?"

"He landed, but we escaped before he could find us."

"Be careful. The Galactic Republic and the Tolarions will soon be at war."

"We'll be all right. These Talokian ships are much faster than either side's."

"I'll see you soon. Keep moving, we'll catch up to you."

"We're going to need food and supplies soon."

"We have enough onboard here. Use the jamming device if you have finished it, and stay out of sight until we reach you. See you shortly. Over and out."

Zarcon had no assurance the Republic would welcome him with open arms.

He just hoped they would listen to his side of the story. He had great confidence in the council, even though he didn't agree with their decision to make Riona the president. He knew, however, they were diplomats first, even though their leader was not. If he was able to approach them before Riona, he might have a chance to help and leave their enemies far behind. From the way Jeff described this new race's vessel, they could reach Sentros in no time at all.

Another thing puzzled Zarcon. Jeff spoke of an evolutionary process that changed the Talokians. He wondered how a race could suddenly go through such a process and what prompted them to do such.

That was the least of his worries. He still didn't know how he was going to tell the council what happened. He could explain that they escaped Belor because of the death ray that Riona stole, but couldn't explain the attack on the Tolarion base on Lingwort. That was something Jeff was going to have to explain, and they didn't usually give credence to explanations from outsiders.

As time slowly passed by, the lingworts felt a sense of joy and relief that they found out their friend was still alive. They found it remarkable he endured his ordeal virtually unscathed. They were looking forward to their reunion with the human.

Zarcon checked the scanners for enemy craft, and then turned towards his friends. "The Federation will be pleased to hear that their tyrannical leader has finally lost his mind," he said. "I've been expecting this for quite some time."

"Will they try to stop him?" Dormiton asked.

"Yes," the arthropod answered. "But they still will not be able to correct what has begun even through diplomacy."

"What is that?" Milgic asked. "Diplomacy?"

"It is learning to communicate with one another; to talk with them," Zarcon explained.

"Like we do?" Dormiton stated.

"Yes, but a little bit different. We have people who represent all of us, and they do the talking. Their war has just begun. I'm afraid however; it might already be too late to stop it."

"Then we have failed," Dormiton said.

"Not quite. There still is a chance."

"A chance at what?" Milgic snarled. "If war has already broken out, how can we stop it?"

"An intergalactic plea for both governments to stop."

"The Tolarions won't stop!" Milgic yelled.

"That is true," Zarcon sighed. "But they will still give in to the Republic's demands if they see how much they have to lose. Their army is not as formidable as ours."

"Now you're talking like Jeff!" Dormiton snapped. "Isn't there a way to solve this without more violence?"

"I'm afraid not, Dormiton. Freedom cannot be weighed by peaceful

87

options," Zarcon replied.

"How did we ever get ourselves into this mess?" Milgic questioned, and held his hand on his face in remorse.

"You didn't, the Tolarions did. You were forced into this war, as was I, which is all the more reason to defend ourselves. When we get to Sentros, I'm sure the council will understand this, and be more than willing to help. They commend peaceful societies such as yours."

"After we explain the situation, can't we just but out?" Milgic suggested. "I'd prefer to go back to Masgria."

"There may be no Masgria to go back to," Zarcon stated. "I'm afraid your quiet little planet is in the middle of this whole thing."

"Why?" Dormiton asked. "We've done nothing!"

"There is something there the Tolarions want, something extremely valuable to them."

"I don't know what that could be," Dormiton said.

"Well let's find out, shall we?" Zarcon said, as he turned towards the computer for consultation. "Computer?"

"Working," it answered.

"Name planets involved in Tolarion operations and indicate the nature of those operations."

"Aria Four, mining operations, Tetra Two, defensive operations, Ulta, mining operations, Caraz, defense operations, Vartos, scientific operations, Valtar, scientific operations."

"Stop," Zarcon interrupted the device. "Indicate planet that is located in star sector 89101, coordinates 69102."

"Ventros."

"Indicate Tolarion interest."

"Scientific operations."

"Nature of operations?"

"Mental expansion experimentation."

"Specify."

"Telekinetic and telepathic research."

"So that it explains it, "Zarcon said, as he turned towards his friends. "They were using the base for some kind of mind experiments."

"Why our planet?" Milgic asked.

"I don't know," Zarcon answered. "Maybe there's some kind of substance there that enables them to read minds."

"I thought that was an ability only your people and Riona possessed," Dormiton stated.

"So did I," Zarcon said. "Computer, is there any substance on Ventros that enables one to possess telekinetic or telepathic powers?"

"Affirmative. A substance known as Triachilite," the machine answered. Zarcon knew Riona's powers were not inherited, but he never expected anything like this. It seemed unfathomable to believe that he either stole this substance or was in league with the Tolarions.

A warning from the computer came up after they closed in on the Beta Four star system. "Asteroid belt in approximately nine hundred thousand miles," it said.

"Turn on shields!" Zarcon yelled. The two lingworts jumped in their seats and strapped themselves in. They knew what to do from Jeff's teachings. "Cut to sub interstellar speed. Brace yourselves!"

They passed through the belt, and the ship slowed to sub interstellar speed. Zarcon carefully guided the ship through it, avoiding many of the smaller asteroids that came at them. When he saw a large asteroid coming right for them, he addressed the computer.

"Avert forty fives degrees!" he yelled. The computer responded, but too slowly. "Switch to manual control!" The computer turned navigation over to him, and Zarcon pressed the navigational controls, but was unable to compensate in time. The asteroid slammed into the side of the antimatter chamber, causing a large explosion on their right side, and started a fire within the back of the ship

"Fire!" Dormiton yelled, as he unbelted himself, and ran to put it out. Zarcon checked the controls, making sure that other systems were operable.

"At least we have life support," he said. "Shields have failed, and the engines are dead."

"How long have we got before there's no air?" Milgic asked, extremely worried.

"About four hours," Zarcon answered. "And we're still far from any Republic outposts."

"What are we going to do?" Milgic cried.

"Well," Zarcon said. "Don't panic for one. And whatever gods you pray to, you better start praying to them."

Three and half hours passed since the incident, and they began to wonder if there was any hope for them. Zarcon couldn't repair the ship; part of the engine had been ripped right out, leaving a hole in the ejection chamber floor. Fortunately, there was another door that separated them from it. As a last resort, he opened communications again, hoping someone would hear him.

"Sentros," he gasped. "This is Zarcon, please come in." There was nothing but silence, as he watched his two lingwort friends begin to suffocate. He then fell unconscious onto the helm. While Zarcon drifted in and out, he heard the main door hatch opened by a laser blast. The door was kicked open, and he could barely make out the figure of a human bending over his slumped body.

"Zarcon," Jeff said, as he helped him breathe in oxygen from a tank. "Are you okay?" He nodded as he awoke.

"Here I thought I was going to rescue you," he said. "You cut off your facial hair." Jeff smiled and helped him to his feet. The Talokians helped the lingworts wake up as well. Dormiton was a little startled to see their faces had changed, and they no longer had claws, but fingers.

"Do not be afraid, Friend," Barva told him. "Our kind will no longer harm you. You have our sincerest apologies. We have undergone complex changes that you wouldn't understand."

When the lingworts regained their senses and saw their friend, they ran to hug him.

"At least you're alive," Dormiton cried. "We were worried sick about you! Hey, you cut all the hair off your face!"

Jeff smiled again and scratched his face while two more Talokians entered the ship. They began to work on the ship's controls. Jeff turned to his arthropod friend. "I'm afraid I lost my laser," he said. "Are there any more on board?"

"Yes," Zarcon answered. "In the weapon compartment. I have some interesting news for you. Our Tolarion friends have been using the Lingwort's planet for mind experiments. Apparently, they are trying to discover the secret to Riona's power."

"It figures," Jeff said. "Balta spoke of domination of the galaxy, and I wouldn't put it past him to use mind control. At least now he's dead."

"Do you know that for sure?" Zarcon asked.

"No, I don't," Jeff answered. "But I very much doubt he survived the attack."

"Nonetheless, the Tolarions are still preparing for attack. We have to reach Sentros soon, or there won't be anything left to control. They'll destroy each other. What are they doing to the ship anyway?" He referred to the Talokians dismantling the helm.

"They're taking the jamming device, and anything else they need," Jeff answered. "We need to destroy this ship when we leave. What about your death ray. Won't that scare the Tolarions off?"

"I don't think so," Zarcon said. "Riona has it by now."

"Then we're in real trouble."

"I'm afraid so," sighed Zarcon. "Knowing him, he's liable to use it against the Republic as well."

"Can the federation stop him somehow?" Jeff asked his arthropod companion.

"That is doubtful. Riona probably will destroy them."

"Do they possess a force field around their planet," Barva asked.

"No," the insect answered. "Only surface defense systems. I take it your culture is much more advanced?"

"Forgive me," Jeff said. "I've forgotten to introduce you. Barva, this is Zarcon, Dormiton and Milgic. They are the friends that I spoke of."

"How do you do," Barva said, as he bowed. "I understand that your races are going through the same ordeal that we went through millions of years ago?"

"That is correct," Zarcon stated. "We're involved in a war. I now know, however, that the Republic is not responsible for our plight. It is Riona!"

"Ah yes," Barva sighed. "The one Mr. Walker spoke so highly of."

"Yes," Milgic answered as he stomped his feet. "He started this mess!"

""Where is he now?" Zarcon asked, unable to register his thought transmissions.

"He has retreated to a distant world," Barva stated. "He has eliminated the rest of his fleet and his crew is next." Zarcon looked at him in awe, as he realized he also had telepathic abilities, and much more advanced as well.

"We have to get to Sentros," Zarcon said. "They will know how to handle the situation. They have probably already sent advisors to Alokia."

"If what you say about Lingwort is true," Jeff suggested. "We need to find out more about the Tolarion mind experiments. They may be the key to his power."

"I hope you're right," Zarcon said. "At least then we have a chance. At any rate, I still need to clear my name of the Zelorion incident."

"Agreed," Jeff said. "Perhaps the council knows more than we do."

"They do have spies on Tolaria," Zarcon informed them. "If they know something, however, they may not tell us."

"Then we'll have to find out on our own," Jeff said. "Unless we can make them understand the situation."

"If it means stopping Riona from using the death ray," Zarcon explained. "They'll be more than willing to help."

They proceeded to switch ships, and prepared for entry into the Republic's space sector as well. They noticed several of their spacecraft on the scanners, but they weren't heading towards them. They were heading toward the Tolarion space sector, probably on route to greet the Tolarion fleet. It was quite obvious to Jeff and his friends that negotiations had fallen through. Even if they explained their situation, there wasn't any guarantee they could stop the violence that already erupted.

Riona's plans for the death ray were still a mystery to them. They knew he had an animosity towards the Tolarions, or was this just a smokescreen to cover the fact he was actually working with them all along? Was he going to use it against anyone who got in his way, including the Tolarions? Jeff and Zarcon had their well justified suspicions he was working with them, and this was just an act.

After the alterations to the new ship were completed, they named it 'Varcon' after a Talokian word meaning 'freedom fighter', and plotted a course for Sentros. With the earth-like world only one day away, they knew they would soon be in Republic territory. They probably wouldn't attack the Varcon right away because it was an alien ship unfamiliar to them. They would investigate first and try to establish contact. Barva turned on the distress signal on board to catch their attention.

The derelict Rigil Four was now floating in space, until they were at a safe distance to fire the main plasma weapons at the craft, leaving it in pieces. Maybe if the Tolarions found their craft in ruins, they would give up their search for Jeff, if they hadn't already. The Republic ships became more frequent as they approached Sentros. Most of them paid no attention to the Talokian ship, after all it wasn't Tolarion and it was too far away still to pose a threat. A couple of scout ships finally noticed them, and came closer to investigate. "Alien ship, identify yourself," a voice announced. Zarcon felt it would be best if he answered, being a Republic officer.

"This is Zarcon, President of Belor," he stated. "We have important news for the high council."

"If you are who you say you are," the voice said. "Then why are you traveling in an alien ship?"

"I can't disclose that information over this frequency," Zarcon explained. "If you like, we will surrender the ship into your custody until we reach Sentros."

"I'll have to clear that with the command center first," the voice said. "Please standby." Within a few minutes, the voice came back with a reply. "Please proceed," the voice said. "We will escort you to Sentros, but please be warned that any hostile actions will not be tolerated."

The group of outlanders followed their orders, and their ship slowed down to sub-orbital speed and proceeded towards the bluish-green planet, which was now within full view. Zarcon could tell that the council would listen to him. After all, they would not let them approach if this hadn't been the case.

The craft penetrated the Nitrogen based atmosphere and they knew for the first time since leaving Ventros they would be safe. Riona wouldn't dare attack Sentros, and if he did, the Republic would surely hunt him down. They were outposts all over the galaxy, and if one of them was destroyed, another would retaliate. Even the Tolarions knew this, and carefully planned around the fact.

Approaching the land masses of the world, they could see immense cloud covers and the structure of their enormous cities. It reminded Jeff of the old pictures he saw of New York City before the nuclear war. He wondered if all their inhabitants were different races of aliens, or all one race. Even Zarcon had never been here before, and was anxious to see what kind of world it was.

They followed the small scout ships as they headed towards one of the metropolises. They could hear the voice of one of its pilots, who contacted headquarters

"Scout Ship Tentra to base," he said. "Please come in."

"Sentros Central here," another voice answered.

"I'm bringing in the visitors," the pilot said. "Over?"

"Proceed, Tentra. Is President Zarcon among them?"

"Affirmative. Bring the whole crew to the council. They are expecting them. Over?"

"Acknowledged. Preparing to dock. Please stand by with security personnel. Over and out."

The three ships came closer to Sentros Central, which possessed buildings which were very similar to those of ancient Rome. It was very clear to Jeff that they took pride in their architecture, as did the Belorions.

The doors were already open when they approached the landing deck. It was apparent that the atmosphere was breathable, for several Sentrons walked back and forth outside the complex. Much to Jeff's surprise and joy, they were mostly humans. 'Finally,' he thought. 'I get to talk to my own kind.'

The Varcon was surrounded by several guards upon landing. Zarcon and Jeff emerged from the main door hatch first, with their arms outstretched. They were directed down a large corridor of the complex.

"Do you think they'll believe us?" Jeff asked Zarcon, as he peered at their captors, which hid behind their helmets and grey uniforms.

"If I can convince them Riona is responsible for Zeloria," Zarcon stated. "It should be easy when they discover what he has done." When they approached the council chambers, the guards opened the cathedral type doors, revealing a long table.

"The Council awaits," Zarcon stated, as they were pushed to enter.

One of the figures rose from the table. He was humanoid in appearance, had no facial hair other a mustache, and very little on the top other than a few grayish black hairs around his ears. He was a hefty gentleman, and wore a long red cloak. He walked towards the insect, which he only had seen through visual communication meetings.

"Zarcon," he said, outstretching his arms in acceptance. "I'm pleased to finally meet you face to face; although I'm sorry it's under these circumstances."

"Hello, Balar," Zarcon answered and embraced him. "You know that I'm innocent."

"Why don't you explain what happened on Belor?" Balar asked. "And you must introduce me to your friends."

"Yes," Zarcon said. "This is Jeff Walker, from a planet called Mars. These two amphibian beings are from Ventros, and these are the Talokians, led by Barva."

"This planet called Mars supports humanoids?" Balar asked.

"Yes," Jeff answered. "My parents were originally from Earth."

"You must have traveled a great distance," Balar said. "I've never heard of either of those planets, or the Talokians for that matter."

"We're both from another universe," Jeff explained.

"Ah," he sighed. "You must have gotten here by way of a Tolarion dimensional transportation device?"

"As far as I know, that seems to be the case. I don't know why though."

"You must have somehow been trapped in a wormhole with them," Balar retorted. "Well, my friends, why don't you take your seats. We have many things to discuss. I held off going to Alokia for negotiations until I could speak with all of you. Barva, your friends are welcome to use the recreation area while we meet."

The five former renegades walked over to the empty seats of the conference table and sat down, as the other Talokians followed the guards out of the room. A feeling of uneasiness came over Jeff as he stared at the various aliens at the table. He could see there was another Belorion at the table, as well as another reptilian being who was completely different from his friends. There were also several beings that were unlike anything else he ever saw before. There was a bluish colored humanoid with wings, a small grayish creature with large dark almond shaped eyes similar to those reported on Earth in the past, and even a cat-like being.

"The session of the council of Galactic Republic of Peaceful Civilizations will now come to order," Balar announced, as he sat down. "Zarcon, you have allegedly attacked a Zelorion outpost with the planetary disintegration device, starting a confrontation with the Tolarions, destroyed a Galactic Republic outpost, and conspired with President Riona in these charges. Do you deny any of allegations?"

"Yes, Sir," Zarcon said, rather surprised at his turnabout behavior. "I deny all of them?"

"If you deny these allegations, how can you account for the incidents that have taken place?" Balar asked.

"Riona is the one you are looking for!" Jeff said, defending his friend. "He is the one who did all of these things!" The reptilian creature spoke to Balar in his native tongue, who interpreted what he said.

"If this is so," Balar asked. "How come he hasn't been found?"

"He's escaped with your device," Jeff said. "He's been trying to hunt us down."

"Although we would like to believe you," Balar stated. "We have no evidence to prove what you're saying. All we have are two destroyed planets, and a missing weapon. Riona has been troublesome with us in the past, but he has never committed an open act of aggression."

"There's always a first time," Jeff smirked, as he smiled to his two amphibian friends.

"Neither have I," Zarcon explained. "You don't really believe I would kill my own people, do you?"

"Of course not," Balar said. "We are merely suggesting that something went on there, and we would like to know the details."

"Riona wanted to know where my home planet was," Jeff said. "Balta also wanted to know this before he destroyed my friends' home. I wouldn't tell him, so Riona destroyed Zeloria instead. He wanted to have Zarcon executed for some reason, and make him appear guilty. Why did they want to know where Mars was?"

"I do not know, but if what you say is true," Balar stated. "This conflict between the two of you has cost us interstellar peace, Zarcon. If he is still alive, and has the weapon like you say, he needs to be found before he destroys us all."

"I believe there's more to it than that, Sir," Zarcon said. "He is apparently trying to get the Tolarions to do his dirty work."

"What does he have to gain from this? "Balar asked, scratching his mustache.

"Plenty," Jeff said. "When both forces have destroyed each other, he'll move in and take over what is left. The Tolarions are planning something with a substance that enables them to have telepathic and telekinetic powers such as Riona's."

"Triachilite," the Belorion ambassador said. "It was first used on Zacharas. That is how we first achieved our mental powers. The drug is absorbed in the genes, and passes down through them, but only if it's administered right. The Belorions learned to control its properties for practical purposes, not for mind control and domination."

"How come you didn't tell us this?" Jeff asked Zarcon, as he turned towards him, feeling a little slighted.

"Because I don't know much about Zarcharian history," Zarcon retorted. "I left there when I was young, and spent most of my life on Belor."

"If they've developed the Triachilite," Balar surmised. "Then we have much bigger worries. As Valtar has told us, the Belorions have achieved a usefulness of the drug, but an addiction to it does have drawbacks, as you have seen in Riona. We had no idea this is where he got his mental powers. At least now we have an avenue to defeat him. There is an old saying; with power comes corruption."

"My people had a similar saying," Jeff responded.

"Is there anything the council can do?" Zarcon asked.

"We can try opening communications with Tolaria," Balar said. "They may not speak to us, but even they do not want an outright war on their hands. If we withdraw, they might also."

Balar walked over to a screen and pressed a button, turning the screen on. A human appeared on it, which totally surprised Jeff as he stood from his seat in shock. He was a white man with black hair, brown eyes, and a full beard. His face was rather thin, and his hair was curly.

Jeff recognized his face right away from Earth history books. It was Dr. Louis Avery, a scientist who first developed cloning experiments on human beings. So this was the Earth man the computer spoke of. It all began to make sense to him. That was why the Tolarions all looked the same, because they were the same, through cloning. That didn't explain, however, why Balta was more superior to the rest, however.

He read that Avery was working on the idea of a superior race of human in the late 2050's, and the experiment went terribly wrong. Abominations were created that had to be destroyed. He was then committed to a mental hospital, only to escape the institution and never be found. Could it be that he somehow discovered how to bend space and time and travel to the future? And if so, why would he do this? Was it because he needed something in this universe that he couldn't find in his own to complete his experiments?' These questions were all going through Jeff's mind, and he was eager to find the answers. While he pondered, the human spoke. "Akros," Balar announced.

"Yes, Balar," he said, annoyed. "What do you wish to discuss?"

"Akros, I want you to break off your attack," Balar answered. "We will withdraw our ships immediately if you do the same. There has been a grave mistake by our leader. He has been ousted from power. I am in command now."

"I am a reasonable man, Balar," Akros said. "But I cannot ignore the fact that you have destroyed two of our bases. I'll tell you what. You turn over the Martian and his accomplices, and we shall be more than willing to negotiate."

"What do you want with the Martian?" Balar asked.

"He has destroyed our bases on Ventros and Zeloria, and has cost us much research!"

"Research of a drug known as Triachilite, perhaps?" Balar tested.

"I know of no such drug," Akros lied. "I will give you two days to comply, or we will attack your planet!" The screen went blank, and the council members' eyes were all fixed on Jeff.

"It appears that the Tolarions want you pretty bad, Mr. Walker," Balar said.

"Yes," he answered. "I guess I've been a bit of a naughty boy!"

"Just what did you do to the Ventros base?" Balar asked.

"Nothing really, just protected my friends from invaders," Jeff said. "I think there may be another reason. I know your Akros."

"How," Zarcon asked.

"He was an Earthling that somehow got here," Jeff explained. "He was working on cloning experiments. I think he wants my DNA."

"It's a possibility," Balar agreed. "But why yours and not just any human?"

"Because I am a descendent of Earth."

"He'll want an answer soon. I have to save our people from war as well."

"Yes, I know," Jeff stated, as he bowed his head in despair. "I'll surrender myself to them."

"No," Dormiton pleaded. "You can't do that!"

"Do I have any other choice?" Jeff asked.

"It would appear not," Zarcon stated.

"You're not going alone!" Dormiton pleaded. "We're all in this together! If we must fight together, we must die together!"

Zarcon addressed him in amazement. "Fight together?" he asked. "How would you know about fighting?'

"I've seen enough to know that I won't give up that easily," he roared. "You can't just let him go in alone!"

"Dormiton's right," Barva agreed. "We must stick together. Besides, I may have a plan."

"Yea," Milgic added. "He's got a plan!"

"Well," Zarcon said, bewildered. "We're going to need one. It would appear the decision has been made. However, there still is the problem of Riona. I will have to deal with him, he's my problem."

"He is all of our problems," Balar said. "And as soon as we can establish peaceful relations again, he will be dealt with."

"How do you know the Tolarions will stick to their word?" Barva asked.

"Because they have in the past," Balar answered. "Our treaties are what keep us alive. That and our highly advanced weapons."

"Which Riona now possesses," Zarcon added. "We must stop him before he causes anymore damage."

The reptilian ambassador spoke into the council leader's ear. "One step at a time," Balar said. "We must first see to it that no enemy vessels penetrate our sector of space. Then, we can negotiate."

"Koros is right," the Belorion member said. "We must defend ourselves first!"

"If we can escape Akros," Zarcon suggested. "We may be able to find out more about the Triachilite."

"That was part of my plan," Barva added, as Zarcon looked a little annoyed by his intellectual superior.

Balar nodded. "Yes," he said, and held his index finger up. "That may be our only chance."

"There hasn't been a cell that can hold us yet," Jeff laughed.

"It will be more dangerous than you can imagine," Balar warned them. "You may all be killed."

Jeff smiled, his brown eyes staring ahead at the new leader of the Republic. "There's an old Earth saying," he said. "We've made our bed, and now we have to sleep in it."

CHAPTER NINE

Riona had given up trying to capture them; it was too late for him to stop them from meeting with the council, and besides, there was other business to attend to. He decided to direct his efforts on his new destination, which remained a mystery to his crew until they finally reached it.

Halfway across the galaxy, a dark figure loomed over his throne and pressed the button to shut off his viewing screen. He sat in the large conference room, and stared at his subordinate. The screen came on and Balar's face appeared.

"We are prepared to meet your demands, Akros," he said. "The renegades will be handed over to you."

"Very good," the ruler sneered. "Bring them to Alokia. They will be transported from there. When they are in our custody, we will withdraw our ships."

"Agreed," Balar said, and turned off his viewing screen.

"They're on their way," Akros said, as he turned to his subordinate. A white hand with claws fell upon the table in front of him.

"Excellent," his subordinate said. "My end of the agreement will be honored once they are in my custody."

"As mine will be when I receive the human and the death ray, as we agreed," Akros said as he smiled at the humanoid. "You have served me well, Riona. Ah, you always were my favorite creation. It shall be a pleasure to see you and Balta in control of the galaxy."

"Balta?" Riona questioned. "I thought he was killed by the human?"

"No, not at all. He is waiting on Alokia for his 'assassin.'"

"As long as he doesn't kill him," Riona said, as he smiled. "He is welcome to torture him in any way he wishes, but as for Zarcon, he better leave him to me!"

"He's not to harm him!" Akros snapped at the humanoid. "He's only to bring him here. After I'm through with him, then the two of you are welcome to do whatever you want."

Riona frowned. "The inferiority of the human race," he sighed. "Always showing the hand of mercy."

"Inferior?" Akros questioned. "You're forgetting who created you. Without me, you wouldn't even exist!"

"I'm sorry, Akros. I've been under a little strain lately."

"You'll be under a lot more if you allow them to escape again!"

"Yes, Akros. I mean no disrespect. It's been a pleasure serving under you as well. The Republic has never suspected a thing, until recently."

"Another mistake you have made?"

"The Belorion left me no choice. He was getting suspicious."

"Are you sure it isn't the drug affecting your decisions?"

"No, it's not that at all. Zarcon has outraged me for the last time!" Riona grew hostile, slamming both hands on the table.

"Calm down, friend," Akros said, as he placed his hand on the shoulder of his long blue cloak. "Soon, you'll have the human, and we'll all have the universe to command. I've been waiting for this day for a century; ever since I left that decrepit place called Earth. To think, their conquerors were after a mere planet, when they could have ruled an entire universe. Excuse me, both universes-yours and mine. Once you know the renegades are in custody, have our fleet attack Sentros."

"Why don't we just use the planet destroyer?" Riona asked, impatient to end this whole fiasco.

"Just because we have it, doesn't mean we have to use it. Haven't you and Balta learned yet? It's about control, not extermination. We want them to know we have it, but put enough fear into them that they will surrender."

"Shall I join him on Alokia?"

"Can you handle the situation without bungling it up?"

"You can count on it! They won't escape me again! What about the others?"

"You can kill the other beings with him; they are no use to me." The door opened as they walked out of the room. Akros turned towards him as they left. "You may go there, but I'm warning you Riona. If I hear that they've escaped again, you'll be terminated just like they will be." Riona grew angered, and grabbed his neck.

"Do not threaten me, Human!" he snarled. "You made me, and I can destroy you just as easily!" Akros' men immediately came, and drew their lasers at Riona. He released his grip, lowered his hand and smiled. Akros straightened his collar.

"And you remember," he said. "I gave you this power, and I can take it away! Your powers are only temporary, and you are as expendable as any other spy."

Riona stormed down the hallway, using his mind to open the doors at the end of the corridor. He was mad at Akros, but he knew he couldn't kill him, not yet anyway. He marched towards the hangar deck, his anger shifted towards the renegades he now would deal with. Balta was his only close friend and the only one who knew what they both envisioned for their future. They didn't need Akros or any human to run the universe. The two of them could do it with the help of his army. When he found out it was the human who tried to kill Balta, it made him even more enraged, but he would have to contain his anger for now. After he brought them to Tolaria, he'd deal with them in his own way.

Back on the planet Sentros, the small renegade crew made preparations to depart to Alokia. Balar described the planet as being a warm hostile, barren world which was used as a Tolarion slave outpost. Slaves were either sent there until they either died or were transported somewhere else.

The atmosphere was very similar to Earth, which was mostly Nitrogen, and nearly 20% oxygen, enough to support life, but the warm barren winds of the planet made it way too dry for water. The other elements were too varied to name, and many were in minute amounts, except for large deposits of minerals such as iron and carbon. Tolaria and Alokia were hardly breathable to humans, because the Oxygen was thick. This explained why on a planet similar to Earth, the Tolarions wore masks to survive. What Jeff couldn't understand is how Akros dealt with this situation. He was breathing the same air as them but he didn't have a mask on. Maybe he was in an air contained facility, a clone himself, or his genetic structure had been altered somehow.

Even though Jeff knew he had placed his friends in great peril by surrendering, he felt it would be the best solution to ending this war. He had a feeling the Tolarions wouldn't keep up their end of the bargain; treaty or no treaty, they didn't seem to him the type to keep their word. Besides, he didn't intend to give up without a fight. He remembered something Zarcon told him on Beloria. He mentioned something about a main control center located on Tolaria. If they were able to get that far, he could plant a bomb there. That wouldn't solve the problem of dealing with Riona however.

As the Talokian ship departed from the Earth-like world of Sentros, Jeff explained to his crew who Akros was a pretty firm feeling of what happened to Mars. If the Tolarions found the base, it and what he did and they began to realize what kind of race he created. He had would have been easy for them to destroy such a vulnerable target. Even if some of his kind escaped, they would die because there wasn't another habitable planet within at least twelve light years.

And what of Lori? If they attacked, she was either a slave for them or already dead. She could be a strong woman and might be able to handle the labor, but she was not trained to endure torture. It upset him to think what became of his friend and realized that going back there was just no longer an option. That would be fine with him, as long as they sent him back to where there were human beings.

Alokia was about two weeks from them by the Tolarion standard of travel. They didn't move there quicker because they needed time to formulate a plan. The Tolarion sector of space was much closer, about three days away. They were notorious for invading neutral territories, and they showed this by landing on Ventros, Zeloria, and Pluto. Zarcon knew they would probably be captured long before they reached their destination.

They watched Sentros fade from sight, and the Varcon casually glided the through the endless region of space. They knew this could be their only chance to save all their worlds from destruction. It was now they needed to come up with a real plan.

"We need to get to the main control center," Jeff said, as he turned away from the viewing screen. Barva brought three of his men with them to help pilot the craft, as it was beyond any of the others' knowledge. "If we can sabotage it somehow, we'll stop them in their tracks."

"What about this Triachilite?" Barva asked. "If they mass produce it, every Tolarion will know what we're up to."

"Then we'll have to find their labs, and destroy them too," Jeff said.

"There's another way," Zarcon remarked. All of their heads turned towards the ambassador. "If we can get to their main control center, we can destroy their entire planet."

"How?" Barva asked.

"By self destructing the ray gun," Zarcon replied. "The explosion would start a fusion chain reaction and incinerate the atmosphere."

"First we have to find the ray gun, and that's assuming Riona even went to Tolaria with it," Jeff said. "We still don't even know if he's working with them or against them."

"I don't know," Zarcon suggested. "I have a feeling there is more to our friend than meets the eye."

"Such as?" asked Barva.

"An alliance with the Tolarions, of course," Zarcon answered.

"Riona?" Dormiton asked. "A spy?"

"Why not," Jeff said. "I mean, where is he now? Certainly not chasing us anymore!"

"Yes," Barva said. "That would explain why he wanted his 'planet destroyer' so badly."

"Do you honestly think that it is on Tolaria," Jeff asked.

"Why not?" Zarcon asked. "Tolaria is located at a strategic area of this galaxy. He can destroy any planet he wishes from there."

"I had no idea its range is so great," Barva said. "What form of power does it use?'

"Fusion," Zarcon stated. "It can even be sent through a wormhole to hit a target. That is why we have never let it fall into enemy hands, and that is why the Tolarions never invaded us before."

"Crude, but effective," Barva remarked. "So why haven't they attacked Sentros yet?"

"I don't know," Zarcon said, annoyed again by his superior attitude. "There has to be a reason. Perhaps they're waiting until after they get us."

"If we can sabotage the main control center," Jeff questioned. "What will happen?"

"It will destroy most of their base," the arthropod answered. "It'll slow them down, but it won't stop them completely."

"Will it hurt them enough for the Republic to effectively attack them," Jeff asked.

"Yes," Zarcon answered.

"Okay then," Jeff surmised. "When we get to Tolaria, we'll have to find a means for escape."

"That won't be easy," Zarcon stated. "Their prisons are extremely well guarded."

"Do we have any other choice?" Jeff asked.

"I guess not," Zarcon stated. "Even if the Republic goes to war, there's no telling of the outcome. There are seven hundred Tolarion bases in this galaxy alone."

"Through cloning no doubt," Jeff remarked.

"Then how can destroying one base make a difference?" Milgic asked.

"Because it is their main base that matters," Zarcon said. "The other bases would be total chaos without Akros running them."

"Is he that powerful a man?" Milgic asked.

"I'm afraid so," Zarcon said. "He's worse than Riona."

"He's the father of creation," Jeff jested. "He's cloned an entire race of beings! Less than perfect, I might add. He forgot the extra eye on them."

"That's how he's been able to have such an enormous population," Zarcon explained. "They must have been all created from the same cell."

"There's a possibility that those cells may be part human," Jeff stated. "Probably from Dr. Avery himself."

"If that is true," Barva added. "Their brain patterns are similar to his. That would explain why they follow his orders explicitly. We went through a similar process with you, although much more complicated."

"And if he was mentally ill like I have read, then maybe his genes were mutated somehow to form these 'Tolarions,'" Jeff responded. "And maybe that's why he still needs me. To correct the process so he can be human again."

"And that would also explain why he needs the Triachilite," Zarcon replied. "He probably needs it for some kind of mind meld with the others."

"Well," Jeff said. "For some time we'll be under confinement. I want us to all stick together, if we can. During this time, we'll have to figure out a way to escape and destroy their base on Tolaria. It sounds like their plan is to transport us from Alokia to Tolaria. I want no heroics while we're there, even if we are separated, okay? We're just going to be transported from Alokia to their main base on Tolaria."

"What if Riona is there?" Dormiton asked.

"Then he is under orders, and probably won't kill us," Zarcon stated.

"Probably?" Milgic doubted.

"Zarcon," Jeff asked, as he changed the subject. "Is there an arsenal on Tolaria?"

"Yes," he answered. "Near the main control center."

"How convenient," Jeff jested. "We should have no problem protecting ourselves once we reach it."

"Five of us against a whole army?" Zarcon questioned. "You're as mad as Riona!"

"You don't have much faith in your own people, do you?" Barva asked.

"My people are of honor!" Zarcon barked. "They will not attack unless a treaty has been violated!"

"And what treaty may that be?" Barva quipped. "They've already destroyed one of your colonies, as well as their own."

"And the Republic will place sanctions on their government," Zarcon surmised.

"That's not enough!" Jeff snapped. "They must pay for what they've done to all of us! I can't understand what's got into you, Zarcon."

"I'm beginning to realize that the Lingworts are right and that war is not the answer. Too many lives have been lost already!"

"And many more will be lost if we don't take some kind of initiative," Jeff stated.

"You should have become a military advisor, Jeff," Zarcon jested. "You can be quite persuasive."

"No," Jeff said. "I never liked all the conflict, but we have to do something. So are you with us?" The human raised his fist in the air.

"I'm with you," he said, and placed his closed claw upon Jeff's fist. The others did the same, in a rebellious alliance against their enemies.

Two days passed since leaving Sentros and the Talokian ship proceeded to get closer to its destination without an incident. It would be ridiculous to escape at this point for it would place the whole Republic in jeopardy. They also needed a means to get to the Tolarion base, which they could never do alone without a fleet behind them. They just hoped that Akros wasn't lying about taking them there.

Zarcon explained what he knew of the construction of Tolarion headquarters, even though he'd never been there. What he knew was relayed to the Republic through spies, especially the arsenal and main control center. Few spies had ever escaped from there alive. What information he didn't know, they extracted from the Rigil Four's computers before they abandoned it. They found the location of the Tolarion prison on the map, at least a mile from the main control center, and heavily guarded.

"How are we going to get there without being seen?" Barva asked. "It would appear that we are outnumbered all of the way."

"What about these air ducts?" Jeff asked as he pointed to the map, which was on the viewing screen.

"If they found out we've escaped," Zarcon explained. "They'll flood them with poisoness gas."

"Well that rules that out," Jeff sighed. "What about this entrance here. It appears to be a cargo bay of some kind. If we can get through there, we can reach the main reactor."

"Too many guards there," Zarcon said. "They'll spot us in a minute."

"Not if we come in as cargo," Barva hinted. "Those food crates are four feet high."

"So," Jeff said, not pleased at what he was about to suggest.

"Our amphibian friends are four feet high," Barva said, as the lingworts looked at each other in disbelief. Jeff stared at him in defiance.

"No!" he insisted. "I can't let them do it! What if something went wrong? Besides, how are they going to get to the reactor from there?"

"The cargo is sent through the control center to other destinations. It might work," Zarcon said.

"How will they escape?" Jeff asked.

"Through one of the air vents," Zarcon said. "If they don't see them, they won't flood it with gas. We can then meet them here. "The air duct nearest to the shuttle deck. From there, we can steal a ship if we have to."

"I do not intend to surrender this ship," Barva boldly stated. "My crew will remain here. They will use their minds on the Tolarions to think that they are not here while the rest of us are interrogated."

"Wow!" Jeff remarked. "I didn't know you could do something like that. The more I learn about this multi-verse, the weirder it gets."

"How will the five of us escape without being seen?" Dormiton asked.

"That's the tricky part," Jeff said.

"We'll have to sabotage the alarm system," Zarcon said. "Which is located here-near the prison exit."

"How many guards are on each floor?" the human asked.

"Ten throughout the floor, twenty at the two exits," Zarcon answered.

"Thirty, heh," Jeff sighed. "The odds are steep as hell, but we might be able to pull it off. Will the Republic back us up by attacking the base?"

"I'll find out," Zarcon answered, and walked to the communications console.

"If they don't," Barva said. "My people will. We should have our fleet ready by then."

"Very good," Jeff said. "I still don't like this idea of you two being key points."

"Neither do we," Milgic exclaimed. "I miss Masgria."

"We've got to help though," Dormiton said, as he turned to him. "In any way we can."

"I'm glad to hear you say that," Jeff laughed.

Zarcon contacted the council and informed them of their plans, using a special code the Tolarions couldn't decipher. Balar didn't totally agree, but backed them up nonetheless. He agreed to send several ships to Tolaria after he was certain they arrived there. His timing needed to be crucial, for if they arrived too soon, their attack would be redundant.

"How much longer before we reach Alokia?" the human asked and turned to the viewing screen.

"Forty two hours and twenty three minutes," Barva stated.

"We'll have to put up with their barbaric conditions," Jeff said. "Just do as you're told. Maybe they won't kill us."

"Wishful thought I'm afraid," Zarcon said. "Even if they say there taking us to Tolaria, there's no guarantee they won't execute us on Alokia."

"That's the chance we'll have to take," Jeff said. "If anything goes wrong at Alokia, we'll try to escape."

"The whole plan sounds like suicide to me," Milgic barked.

"Suicide or not, we have no choice," Barva said. "The Talokians will stay out of range of the Tolarions' scanners until they're needed. The homing devices will also link into my people's computers."

"How can a small fleet be effective against Alokia's defenses?" Zarcon questioned.

"Our ships are considerably more advanced than the Republics' or the Tolarions'," Barva said. "We can see them before they can see us, and we can attack from a farther range."

"The scanners indicate three space craft approaching at rapid speed." One of Barva's men said. "They appear to be Tolarion."

"We haven't even entered their sector of space yet," Zarcon cried. "They are going to capture us sooner than expected."

"Prepare to open communications with them," Jeff said.

"Once we leave, follow us, but at a distance," Barva instructed his men as well.

"What if they try to destroy the ship?" Zarcon asked.

"Once we're onboard," Barva said. "Leave here at warp-light speed."

"Your kind has mastered the speed of light," Zarcon asked.

"Not exactly," Barva explained. "We've developed a technology that allows us to bend space and time forming a field around our ship. It's similar to your wormhole generator in this respect. It allows us to surpass the speed of light, but the ship does not move itself, just the space around it."

"Fascinating," Zarcon said. "We can only achieve light speed by wormhole generation. We haven't developed that far yet."

"You soon will," Barva predicted.

"Communications are open," one of Barva's men announced.

"This is Major Jeff Walker, from the Republic," he announced. "We are here to surrender."

Their message was received by the Tolarion ship which answered in English. "I am Kolar, of the Tolarion fleet," the voice said. "Prepare for us to dock and board. Do not attempt any resistance or you will be killed."

"Stop all engines and cut all power except the main door hatch," Barva commanded. They waited in the darkness for their captors, and heard the ship docking along the side of them. There was a loud grinding sound, a loud snap, and the doors locked within each other. The main door hatch opened, and they were greeted by several guards who were wearing air masks on their faces. The beasts immediately grabbed the five of them and put them in the other ship. The other Talokians were invisible to their minds just as Barva said they would be. Before

106

they had time to speak, the one called Kolar grabbed Jeff's arm. "There's someone who wishes to speak with you," he sneered.

Jeff, who thought it was Riona wasn't surprised until he found out who it really was-Balta.

"Balta!" Jeff yelled. The sinister Tolarion leader's smile could be seen through his transparent mask.

"Yes, Mr. Walker," he answered. "It is I. You thought you had done away with me, heh? You'll find that I'm not as easy to kill as you think I am."

"There's no way you could have survived," Jeff said, as he searched for the acid burn on his hand. "Your whole base was destroyed."

"I survived by the skin of my teeth, as you humans say, but I survived. You are very strong willed, Walker. It will be a shame to execute you. You could have had a place in my new empire."

"Right next to Akros, I imagine."

"Akros is a foolish man! He no longer has control over me or my race. I am their leader now, not some human being who is truly inferior to us."

"That's no way to talk about your creator," Jeff jested.

"Touché`, Walker, touché," Balta laughed. "How clever you are! It's a pity you won't live long enough to discover too much more about us. Right now, however, I'm letting you live only because of Akros and have adjusted the air in here for more delicate life forms such as yourselves. Take them in the back!"

The guards obeyed his orders and grabbed the small crew, shoving them in the brig. When they started to push Jeff in, Balta stopped them. "Wait," he said. The two guards turned toward their leader, as he pulled a knife from his belt, and put it against his throat. "I need to repay you for your insolence! You're lucky to be alive. If it wasn't for Akros, you wouldn't be. Nonetheless, I'll give you a reminder of my fury, just like you gave me!" Balta slashed his face quick, just under his eye, as he struggled to escape. Blood dripped down his neck and onto the floor, and the stinging pain was unbearable.

Balta laughed wildly, and waved for the guards to place him in the brig. Dormiton quickly ripped a section of Jeff's pants and placed it against the wound to stop it from bleeding. The group was astonished by his wicked act of cruelty towards their friend.

They left the allegedly empty Varcon in space, and the Tolarions tried to pilot it, but were unable to do so. Balta wanted to take it for research, but because they couldn't pilot it or tow it, they decided they'd have to abandon it. As Alokia came into view the next day, Balta turned towards his crew.

"Prepare to land," he ordered. "Alokia base, this is Balta, can you read me?"

"Yes, Sir," a voice announced. "You are clear to land at sector 291."

"Roger," Balta said. "Landing at sector 291."

The tyrant smiled at the brown barren world, knowing that victory would soon be in his grasp. The Republic wouldn't dare defy him now; not if they wanted to see their delegates alive again. The ship gradually floated into the atmosphere, its retro rockets slowing the ship down considerably. The surface of the planet was covered with a raging dust storm, which gave them great difficulty in landing. It was apparent, however, that the Tolarions were well accustomed to these conditions. The wings of the large Tolarion craft bobbed from the winds of sixty miles an hour upon entering the landing strip area.

Jeff covered his face with the cloth that Dormiton gave him to avoid the flying dust particles, and ripped off more pieces of his pant leg and gave it to the others to cover their faces as well. The air was breathable, but very dirty for humans, and the others weren't used to the weather conditions either. Their landing was rather rough, and several rocks flew toward them, one even bouncing off the nose of the ship. When the Tolarion vessel finally landed, Balta made his way back to the brig. As he opened the door, he grabbed Jeff by the hair and threw him against the wall. The human landed with his back to it, and collapsed on the floor.

"Let's see how you can escape one of our worlds," he laughed, as he grabbed his right arm and pulled him to his feet. "You're lucky if you survive a day or two in one of these storms! Move the rest of them to the workstations, President Zarcon and Walker will come with me!" It seemed to Jeff they only wanted to execute the two of them, and keep the others as slaves on Alokia.

Six of the guards directed the reptilian and amphibians outside to a section of the complex that lay directly in front of them, as Zarcon and Jeff were taken in another direction with Balta and four guards following behind them. They edged their way to the entrance while the bitter winds and abrasive sands beat against them. Jeff was used to the wind and sand, but not the scorching heat. On Mars, there were frequent sandstorms, but he was protected by the insulation of a spacesuit, and temperatures were much cooler.

The two renegades were pushed into the entrance, and the doors slid open. Jeff felt completely helpless, as five laser guns were pointed at them, in case they might try to escape. The inside hall was large and long, and traveled in all directions. They were pushed into a hallway on the right, which led to a room where most of the cargo was kept. Jeff guessed that this was their cargo holding area, mainly due to the tanks and metal crates that were scattered around the area. Jeff thought about ripping the mask off that protected Balta's face, but he knew he was just be shot if he did so. They were led through an area to an elevator which was on the far side. They entered it, and Balta announced their destination.

"Main Control," he said, and the machine responded. When it reached the third floor, the doors opened, and revealed another corridor. They walked to the end of it and the doors opened.

There was a large table, where a blue cloaked figure had his back to them. He turned around to greet them

"Riona!"

"Yes, Zarcon," he laughed. "It's me. You didn't think we gave up looking for you?" Jeff turned towards Balta.

108

"I knew this was a setup," he surmised. "You and Riona were planning Zarcon's execution all along. What did you promise him, Balta, your precious Triachilite?"

"Well, Mr. Walker, I'm impressed. You have done your homework," Riona laughed. "On the contrary, Mr. Walker. I promised him something much better-total rule of the galaxy. Sort of a joint venture, you might say. And with the Belorion death ray, no one will stop us!"

"It's not yours to rule," Zarcon asked. "And what about Akros?"

"What about him?" Riona snarled. "Once we get back to Tolaria, he's a dead man!"

"Where is the death ray?" the insect questioned.

"Do you think we'd be fools enough to reveal that information?" Riona asked. "Balta, can't we dispose of these destitutes?"

"Not yet, Friend," the ape-like creature said. "If Akros wants them alive, we'll give them to him alive. And then we'll kill all three of them, including Akros."

"You would do that to your own father?" Jeff jested.

"Power has no relatives," Balta coldly sneered.

Jeff tried to grab him, but was held back by the guards. "What about our friends?" he asked.

"We have no desire to kill them," Balta explained. "They will remain here as prisoners of the empire, digging the mines for precious metals."

"You are a sadistic son of a bitch, aren't you?" Jeff snarled.

"And you are becoming tiresome, Mr. Walker," Balta hissed. "Put them on board the Starlighter. We'll depart from Alokia in one hour."

The guards grabbed the two prisoners, and pushed them towards the elevator doors. Jeff struggled to get away, but a guard pushed him against a wall. When the elevator doors shut and they left, Balta turned towards his faithful friend

"How did he know about the Triachilite?"

"Zarcon must have told him," Riona answered.

"What else does he know?"

"Nothing other than what the Republic has told him."

"Good. Let's not make any more mistakes. I want them both terminated when we get back to Tolaria."

"It will be my pleasure. What about his friends? Are they really going to the workstations?"

"Of course not. They are being eliminated as we speak."

On the other side of the complex, Barva and his two Ventrosion friends were being led down a corridor, which was considerably below the planet's surface.

They were brought to a dark tunnel and shoved inside. There was a wall at one end, and a solid iron door at the other.

"End of the line," one of the Tolarions said as he slammed the door. Dormiton ran to it, and slammed his fist against it.

"Now what?" Milgic asked.

"We wait," Barva said.

"For what?" Dormiton asked.

"Until they decide what to do with us," Barva answered. "I sense that Zarcon and Jeff will be on their way to Tolaria soon. Security will lighten up a little after they've left, and then maybe we'll stand a chance at getting out of here. They've probably already started sending troops to intercept the Tolarion fleet. The war has already begun."

They sat in the darkness, and heard a hissing sound that grew louder. "Gas," Barva yelled, as they began to choke, smoke entering through vents in the chamber. Dormiton fell to the floor, unconscious. Barva also was queasy, as they heard a laser blast at the door. The door was kicked open, as they fell to the floor. Three humans who wore gas masks helped them to their feet and out of the chamber, passing dead guards that were outside of the chamber. They were directed down a hallway and into an open room, which led to a panel in the wall, which they pushed. The three of them were led to a stairway. At the bottom of the stairway there was a narrow passageway that led to another wall. One of the guards reached his hand in a hole in the wall, and it opened into a doorway. They found themselves surrounded by a group of human beings, which were a resistance group. They carried lasers and also early twenty first century rifles.

A six feet two curly blonde haired man used a damp cloth to revive them to full awareness. He had a rather muscular build, and was in his early fifties.

"Who are you?" Barva asked, as the humans looked at one another, intrigued by these English speaking reptile creatures.

"I'm John Carver," he said. "We are from an installation on a planet called Mars. We were brought here by some creatures called Tolarions, just as you were."

"Did you say Mars?" Dormiton asked.

"Yes," Carver said. "Have you heard of us?"

"Yes," Barva said. "We have a friend from there."

"What's his name?" asked Carver.

"Jeff," Milgic said. "Jeff Walker."

"Walker?" a girl's voice shouted, as she emerged from the crowd. She had curly blonde hair and blue eyes, and was very slender, and seemed very eager when she heard the name. The two lingworts looked at each other in amazement when they knew this was the woman Jeff spoke about on many occasions on the island.

"Is your name Lori Anderson?" Dormtion asked.

"Yes," she said. "Have you seen Jeff? Is he all right?"

"I'm afraid not," Barva sighed. "Balta's got him."

"Are they here, in the complex?" Carver asked.

"I don't know," the reptile said. "My thought transmissions are weak down here. They had orders to take him to Tolaria to be executed."

"Executed?" Lori screeched. "We have to do something!"

"If my calculations are right," Barva said. "My fleet should be arriving here soon to attack this base."

"If that's true," Carver said. "We better get out of here! Our installation down here isn't designed for an attack of such proportions. We'll have to save your friend before Balta gets away."

"Have you ever heard of the Galactic Republic of Peaceful Civilizations, John Carver?" Barva asked.

"Yes," he said. "The Tolarions have spoken of them on several occasions and they have some of their people here as prisoners as well."

"Well," Barva continued. "They are under orders to attack Tolaria once Jeff is brought there. He has a mission to destroy the base. If you can help us with his mission, we'd be forever in your debt."

"Consider it done," another hefty human with grey hair said. "I'm Steve Malone. They have harmed enough of our people as well."

"Our main concern now is getting out of here and to the main hangar decks," Carver stated.

"What about Jeff?" the agitated Lori asked. Carver grabbed her by the shoulders, and looked deep into her blue eyes and consoled her.

"He knows what he is doing," he told her. "If they say he has to be captured, then he has to be captured. Is there a chance we can save him before he is executed?"

"Barva," the reptile said. "My name is Barva. I am second in command of the Talokians. These are my friends Dormtion and Milgic, from the planet Ventros. I don't know, but I do know the location of where he is going."

"It might not be an easy task," Lori said. "They appear to be heavily armed."

"We devised a plan to send these two through the air ducts. If we can get to the main control center, we can self destruct the base. During the confusion, we'll have to find Jeff."

"We'll have to find out where they're keeping him first," added Carver. "Can you contact the Republic?"

"After we get out of here, we should be able to," Barva stated.

"Let's get started!" Carver yelled, and handed a laser to each of them. "Once we reach the hangar decks, protect the ships. They're our only way off this god-forsaken planet."

They ran through the corridor, and could hear weapon blasts that penetrated the outside walls of the base. They ran up the stairs and into the complex, as the base began to fall around them. They were attacked by several Tolarions while they ran down another corridor. The hallways flashed with great light intensity as lasers blasted in all directions. Even the lingworts finally got involved, and fired their lasers at the enemy. When they finally reached the hangar deck, they could see Balta and Riona exiting the elevator. Carver tried to shoot at them but missed Riona just laughed, and they both vanished into the craft, and it started to lift off.

They fired at the Starlighter when it left the hangar deck, but the ceiling began to give way and they needed to get to the other spaceships quick. The catwalks fell to the floor below, destroying machinery and Tolarions as well.

The army of approximately two hundred humans converged on their enemy, and fired their lasers as they headed towards the spaceships. Carver and Lori fired at three Tolarions who tried to escape, and ran to the nearest ship, opening the hatch. Barva, Dormiton, and Milgic ran behind them, and jumped inside in haste. A Tolarion grabbed Dormiton's leg and yanked it, and tried to pull him from the platform outside the ship. He kicked him in the face, regretfully, and his attacker fell to the floor.

He jumped in the ship, and shut the hatch behind him. The other humans followed suit, and grabbed whatever ships they could. Most escaped, but several people were killed in the process, as the base began to collapse around them. John pressed the communication panel and spoke into it.

"I want all ships to rendezvous with the Talokians. Stand by for further orders. Barva, can you speak with your fleet?"

"Certainly," he said, and walked over to the panel. "Talokian fleet, this is Barva. Centar, do you read me?"

"Centar here," a voice answered. "We read you loud and clear."

"Break off attack until we can reach you," Barva ordered. "We will be in Tolarion ships, all except one- the Starlighter. It should be approaching you now. Track him, but don't attack."

"Affirmative," Centar said. "Out."

"The Republic is fully aware of your plans?" Carver asked.

"Yes," Barva answered. "We have met with the council. They informed us they will not attack until Jeff reaches Tolaria."

"Then all we have to do now is follow them," Carver said. "And wait until the order to attack."

Their new Tolarion vessels climbed through the atmosphere until the base was no longer in sight, and the Talokians destroyed the rest of what was left there. The attack had been so sudden the Tolarions didn't expect it, and were unprepared for it. Balta and Riona escaped again and were on their way to Tolaria thinking they had leverage by having prisoners, but had no idea that their whole arrangement with Akros was setting them up for the kill.

When Carver and the others rendezvoused with the Talokians, they boarded the Varcon. It was decided that Carver, Lori, Barva and the two lingworts would pilot it, with both forces following close behind. Balta's ship was completely out of distance at the moment, but they were still locked onto to it, and tracked every movement. The ship could easily overpower its speed, but there wasn't a reason to. They knew exactly where the Starlighter was headed, and didn't want to be detected.

The Republic forces were in position for an attack on Tolaria. Even if the Tolarions were successful in their attack on Sentros, there wouldn't be a home for either of them to return to. If they by some chance constructed another base somewhere else, the Republic was determined not to let this happen again.

It was decided the stolen Tolarion ships would proceed first and catch their forces off guard, then Barva's fleet, and then the Republic's fleet. John Carver was well acquainted with the Tolarions' spaceships and machinery. After all, he spent the last past two years on Alokia, building up a resistance group against them and was quite successful in his efforts. They managed to release many of their prisoners, and their plans were to take over the base; that is until the Talokians arrived. The job was meant for the group, and they saw it was only right to return the favor to Barva's people for freeing them from Alokia. Between the two factions, there was a very prominent invasion force of about fifty ships, with the Varcon leading the way. Barva placed the ship on auto pilot and turned to his friends.

"It will take about a week for them to reach Tolaria at their present speed," he said. "We do have to discuss a plan, however."

"What did you have in mind?" Carver asked. Barva switched on the viewing screen, showing the layout of the complex.

"We were originally going to send these two through the cargo bay area," he said. "But because Jeff and Zarcon were captured, our course must be changed. I think we should land the Tolarion ships in the landing bay area first. We can then take control of that area. Since most of the ships will be engaged in battle with the Republic, that particular area will be undermanned."

"Even if we take control of that area," Lori asked, as she pointed at the screen. "How do we get to here, where the main control center is?"

"The main control center is very close to the landing bay area," Barva said. "If your men can keep them occupied, the three of us can dismantle the security system and eliminate the force field that surrounds the base there."

"What about Sentros?" Dormiton asked, thinking of the humans there.

"I'm sure that the Republic knows its own position," Barva said. "They are probably already taking defensive maneuvers."

"I've seen what the Tolarions are capable of," Lori remarked. "Are you sure that the Republic can defeat them?"

"Yes," Barva answered. "The Republic has more unification. They are more likely to survive. Although, the Tolarions have developed some advances that the Republic has not achieved yet."

"No one wins as far as bloodshed is concerned," Dormiton cried. "Even Jeff has said that at one time or another." Lori smiled at the small amphibian, and put her hand on his cold, leathery shoulder. When she touched the surface it reminded her of a snake.

"You are very fond of him aren't you?" she asked.

"Yes," Milgic said. "We owe everything to him. Unfortunately though, he is the one who also got us into this mess."

"It wasn't him," Barva said. "It was the Tolarions. They came to your planet

113

to produce the drug Triachilite."

"Drug?" Carver yelled and slammed his fist against the wall in anger. "You mean to tell that this whole thing is about a drug?"

"Not just a drug," Barva explained. "A drug that enables its user to have telepathic and telekinetic powers."

"And what do the Tolarions want with it?" Lori asked.

"To be the superior race and to rule every world they can," Barva said.

"You've got to be kidding!" Carver said, and shook his head in disbelief.

"Nonetheless," Barva said. "They are attempting it."

"They are the ugliest, meanest things I've ever seen!" Lori remarked.

"Not to be insulting but to tell you the truth," Barva stated as a matter of fact. "They are everything that the human race has come to be at one point or another. In fact, it was a human who created their race and used defective human genes to do it."

"A human?' Carver asked, bewildered. "Who?"

"A man called Akros. A man you may know as Dr. Louis Avery. I believe that was what Jeff told me his name was," Barva answered.

"Louis Avery!" Lori exclaimed in shock. "He was a scientist in the late twenty first century."

"Genetic engineering," Carver stated. "He was also quite fond of space and time travel theory as well. How did he get here in this universe?"

"Probably the same way we did," Lori surmised. "Through a doorway. He must have discovered the process."

"Not likely," Barva corrected. "Even a genius at that particular time period from Earth couldn't have come up with idea. There must be another answer."

"There must be another race involved," Carver suggested. "Either that or he stole the idea from the Republic somehow."

"That would seem more likely," Barva said. "But even they haven't perfected the wormhole process yet. And that still doesn't explain how he got here in the first place."

"Do we still have a scan on Riona's ship?" Carver asked.

"Yes," Centar said who was also onboard. "They are .054282 light years ahead of us. They still appear to be heading towards Tolaria."

"Any sign of enemy craft?" Barva asked.

"Not yet," Centar answered. "So far we're in the clear."

Dormiton started to reminisce about the days on the island and all of the tribulations they went through thus far, and turned to his friend in sorrow.

"Do you realize this could be the end of us?" he asked and placed his hand on his shoulder. "If we fight, we may be killed."

"Dying," Milgic said. "Is better than going back to a place where we would be slaves. You know that yourself."

"I can't wait to see home again!" Dormiton cried. "I miss the lush green jungles of the island."

"We'll never see home again!" Milgic muttered.

"We will survive, you'll see!"

Although Dormiton believed in his mind his friend Jeff was invincible, he also knew they were up against the toughest challenge they ever faced. At the moment Dormiton thought about something he said one day on the island.

"You will never find your own path in life," he said. "Unless you first put on your shoes and start walking." Dormiton felt in his heart that the days of walking were over and it was time for running-right back home to Masgria.

CHAPTER TEN

Onboard the Starlighter, Riona and Balta amused themselves by interrogating their prisoners. Jeff was exhausted from their mistreatment of him, pushing and shoving that caused him substantial wounds. Balta punched him several times in the face, which caused his left eye to bleed and bruise. "Tell me why you were snooping around our Ventros base, Mr. Walker," Balta sneered.

"I told you the truth, you just don't care if I'm right," Jeff gasped. "You were attacking my friends!"

"You were after the Triachilite," Riona accused.

"No!" Jeff screamed. "No!"

"You lie!" Balta snarled. "You were sent by the Federation as a spy!"

"He's probably been conditioned to mind block me," Riona said. "We're wasting our time. Why don't we just torture his Belorion friend? Then he will tell us."

"Is that what you want, Human?" Balta barked. "For us to torture your friend?"

He was interrupted by his subordinate, Kolar. "We are apparently being scanned, Sir," he said.

"Identify," Barva commanded the computer.

"A Fleet of ships, Tolarion in nature," the computer said.

"Probably escaping from Alokia," Riona said. "Those humans made a mess out of our base."

"What do you know about that?" Balta asked, as he turned towards Jeff. He grabbed the human around the neck firmly.

"Nothing," Jeff gasped.

"You know nothing about another attack of our base, heh," the Tolarion jested. "Very well, have it your way. When we reach Tolaria it won't matter anyway, because you'll both be dead!"

"Is that a promise?" Jeff sarcastically asked. Balta swung his fist, and struck him in the other eye.

Zarcon, who sat next to Jeff, turned towards Balta. "Is that all your people understand is violence?" he asked.

"We will be the true leaders of the galaxy when this is all over!" Balta shouted.

"Dream on," Jeff joked, as he raised his head. He didn't have much energy left.

"And you, Riona," Zarcon scolded. "Is this really worth giving up twenty years with the Republic for?"

"Yes," he laughed. "As a matter of fact, it is!"

"And what happened to our ray gun?" Zarcon questioned. "On Tolaria perhaps?"

"You've said quite enough," Balta said, as he raised his fist to the arthropod.

"Wait," Riona said, as his comrade backed away from the chair. "I've got a better idea. Perhaps you might want some mental anguish, President Zarcon?"

He began to place an image in Zarcon's mind. The belorion visualized hanging by his leg from a tree on his home planet, Zacharas. There was a pool of bubbling lava below him, as the branch began to break. He screamed, as he could feel in his mind the unbearable heat that seared through his whole body. Illusion or not, in his mind it felt real. Riona broke his concentration, as Zarcon could still feel the burning sensation. afterwards

"Does that convince you that we mean business, Zarcon?" Riona laughed. "How about it? Why was the human on Ventros?"

"He's been telling the truth!" Zarcon cried. "The council told us about the Triachilite!"

"The council?" Balta barked. "How did they know?"

"Perhaps they have a few spies of their own?" Riona suggested. "It doesn't matter anymore. Once the weapon is in position, they don't dare defy us!"

"I hope you're right," Balta said. "The Ventros base has been moved, however, and its location remains a secret. Riona, come with me." The two exited the brig and walked towards the control room.

"Do you believe they're telling the truth?" Balta asked.

"Yes, they are," Riona answered. "Zarcon has done nothing to block my thought transmissions, and they have no idea where their friends are."

"Probably tailing us in that alien ship," Balta surmised. "Are you sure that the Triachilite is still working?"

"Of course," Riona assured him. "When we reach Tolaria, I will give you the formula, as we agreed."

"You should have given it to me on Ventros. Maybe then this whole incident could have been avoided."

"I doubt it. They would have found out about it without the human's help. I also wanted to make sure that Akros was dead first."

"He'll be dead when we reach Tolaria," Balta insisted. "I'll see to it personally."

"If you don't mind," Riona chuckled. "I'd like to have the privilege."

"So be it. How long before we reach Tolaria, Sergeant?" Balta asked his helmsman.

"Thirty four hours, Sir," his subordinate answered. "There is a gas cloud coming up that we need to avoid."

"Is that Tolarion fleet still behind us?" Riona asked.

"Yes," the helmsman said.

"Then at least we have some added protection," Balta said. "We'll try to lose them near it."

"If we get too close, it will affect our operating systems, Sir," the sergeant said.

"I'm well aware of that," Balta said. They couldn't detect the Talokian ships due to their advanced jamming systems, which made them virtually invisible to the Starlighter's scanners. Balta was still skeptical about whether it was his own fleet or the rest of the renegades.

The hours passed, and Jeff and Zarcon sat restrained in the brig. They kept their minds on clear thoughts, which was not an easy task for either one of them. Jeff spent most of the time sleeping, which was long overdue. He hadn't really slept a good night's sleep since he was on Zebula. He wondered if there wasn't something he could have done on Pluto to prevent this. Perhaps if he hadn't killed the Tolarion scout or invaded their ship. He knew that being a violent race to begin with, the only way he could have stopped them was to somehow go back in time and stop their creation from the start, which was physically impossible. If they could get close to the ray gun, they might be able to self destruct it. It would start a nuclear blast that would destroy most of Tolaria. As Tolaria came closer, so did their fears. All of this became absent from Jeff's mind, however, as he thought about how simple life was on Lingwort. His only disappointment of the world was the fact there weren't any humans to share it with.

He also knew that if their friends couldn't rescue them, they would surely be executed. The Tolarions didn't take kindly to spies of any sort, especially those involved with the Republic. It was apparent to Jeff now that Beloria and Mars no longer existed. Their people were killed and the bases destroyed. Although only the Zacharians colonized on Beloria, there were at least ten thousand of them. Riona showed no remorse over the mass murder at all.

The Tolarion government killed many more than that, however, and took control of many underdeveloped colonies. The fusion weapon and the Triachilite were indeed the two catalysts the Tolarions needed to achieve their goal. What Riona and Balta would receive in return was beyond either of their imaginations.

The Tolarion fleet dragged behind them as their destination finally became within their reach. The Varcon still remained undetected by the empire itself, working to their advantage. Carver notified the Republic of their position, and the fleet was on stand-by alert. Half of their fleet remained near Sentros for defensive measures, and fought Tolarion ships that already arrived. Although Tolarions were much more aggressive and numerous, they lacked the technology to win this war effectively. Many of the Tolarion ships were being attacked from behind and without warning.

The dark brown world of Tolaria was now within the range of the Starlighter's scanners. The Talokian vessels silently followed behind them, keeping a great distance from them. Balta gazed at his home planet on the screen as he paced across the floor of the control room.

"Tolarion control center," he announced into the ship's communication panel. "This is Balta, please respond."

"This is Tolaria control center," a voice announced. "We read you loud and clear."

"Prepare landing bay for Tolarion fleet," Balta commanded. "We will land in three hours. The fleet is behind me, perhaps an hour or two."

"Roger," the voice said. "Akros wants you to report to him immediately."

"Affirmative," Balta said. "Over and out."

Riona placed his claws on his friend's shoulder. "Akros seems a bit anxious, doesn't he?" he remarked. "It's a good thing we lost the others in the gas cloud."

"I hope you're right. He does seem anxious. Anxious to die," Balta laughed as his crew joined in. "Get the prisoners and bring them up here!"

The crew responded, and four guards walked back to the brig and opened the door. Jeff took a weak swing at one of them as they grabbed his arm and threw him to the floor of the control room. "Still fighting back, heh?" Balta sneered, the guards lifting him back to his feet. "I admire your persistence, Mr. Walker."

Jeff pushed them away and lifted himself up, and they pulled Zarcon out as well. "This is my home," Balta boasted, as the human gazed at the viewing screen. "And it will be your cemetery. You still have a choice, however, if you want to reconsider?"

"Not on your life!" Jeff barked.

"You are stubborn!" the Tolarion said. "That is one of humans' most annoying traits."

"And ignorance and barbarianism are a couple of yours," Jeff responded.

"You're probably still wondering how you ever got in this universe in the first place, aren't you," Balta asked.

"The thought has crossed my mind."

"We brought you here, accidently through the wormhole, after you attacked a ship of ours on Pluto, as you left the Mars base."

"So you do know where Mars is!"

"Yes I do, Mr. Walker, and I've already conquered it," he sneered with terror in his eyes.

"You son of a bitch!" the human yelled, as he violently grabbed for his throat. Two guards pulled him off immediately and held on to him tight. He felt a murderous rage inside him he never felt before.

"It may interest you to know that I am not without pity," Balta explained. "Most of your people have been relocated to various work colonies such as Alokia."

"So they could die a slow death instead?" Zarcon remarked.

"Who is Lori Anderson?" Riona asked, as he read Jeff's thoughts. "A past romantic interest, perhaps?"

"Where is she?" Jeff yelled, as he clenched his teeth and fist and struggled to get away.

"I have no idea," Balta answered. "She could be on any one of one hundred planets, or she could be dead already?"

"I'll kill you!" Jeff roared, his adrenaline pumping through him.

"Don't bet on it!" the Tolarion laughed. "Pretty soon, you'll be the one who dies."

"There is still one thing that puzzles me," he stated, calming down a little.

"What is that?" Balta asked.

"How I ended up on Ventros."

"We brought there and left you for dead," Riona explained. "Your ship crashed into the ocean. We assumed that you drowned."

"I thought you needed my DNA?" Jeff questioned.

"Akros needs it," Balta said. "We don't. We just want you out of our hair."

"I won't be out of your hair until I kill both of you!" the human said, as he continued to struggle to get free.

Two and a half hours later, the retrorockets were fired and the ship entered the nitrous oxide atmosphere. They could gradually see the enormous city that seemed to stretch a continent. It was hard to believe that half of its residents were at battle elsewhere. Jeff kept an undisturbed watch on his captors as they glided towards the metropolis.

The ship was currently entering the landing bay, which was an enormous storage area for supplies and the Tolarion fleet. There was enough room in it to house at least five hundred spaceships. It was similar to an aircraft carrier, for there were landing strips like an airport runway.

The Starlighter landed, and they saw at least fifty guards waiting for them. They were heavily armed, and each one had the same ugly look of conquest in their eye. Riona opened the main hatch, and he was saluted by his welcoming committee. Balta followed him, and the guards brought the prisoners out behind him. "Guard them well," he told his men. "I want them alive until their execution. But first, Akros wants to see them, so we shall not keep his Excellency waiting."

The troop of Tolarions surrounded the two renegades and they were directed down a corridor, their superior officers following them. They headed down a second corridor, which took them in the direction of Akros.

They still wore their masks, which Jeff didn't quite understand. Why was there Oxygen here in the complex? He did find the air heavier than what he was used to on Ventros, but it was still breathable. They were lead down the hallway, and many thoughts raced through Jeff's mind as he realized he still had many unanswered questions.

Would Barva and the lingworts be able to help them in the way Barva had said? Would the Republic come through with their promise and what about this gas cloud? How would it interfere with the Varcon's systems, and would they survive the ordeal? All of this raced through his mind in a matter of minutes.

He was going to finally meet the famous Dr. Louis Avery face to face. It was hard to believe that someone who was so prominent a scientist would resort to such a destruction of any race. The young geneticist and physicist in the history records would never have done this, at least according to what he heard. Something must have happened to him to carry out such a personal vendetta against the human race. He always admired Avery's great achievements, but never pictured him as an adversary. One thing was for sure; if Jeff didn't stop him he would destroy both universes.

CHAPTER ELEVEN

As the Varcon approached the gas cloud, Carver walked up to the helm which was piloted by Centar. Barva was next to him, surveying the scanners. "How long before we reach Tolaria," he asked.

"Two hours," Barva answered.

"Do they know we're following them?"

"No I don't believe so. Being as primitive as they are, they would have attacked us by now."

"Primitive? They were able to destroy two bases and an entire planet!"

"Exactly," Barva said.

"You certainly are one strange being."

"In what way?"

"These Tolarions have spacecraft and weapons that we on Mars had never seen before. They travel through wormholes. How is that primitive?"

"Just because a race has technological achievements, it does not make them an advanced society. Like I stated to your human friend Jeff Walker, a race has not truly achieved enlightenment unless they can use their knowledge for peaceful and productive purposes."

"I see," Carver said. "Makes sense to me."

"What type of energy did Mars use to travel?"

"Ion propulsion, rocket fuels and fission. Slow, but we never really ventured far from our own solar system. We knew over a century ago that there was other life in the universe. We just didn't know how to get there."

"And you still as a human would never understand it. I do not mean to be offensive, but the quantum physics involved are complicated."

"Well," Carver said, slightly hurt. "Remind me to get the crash course when I get back to Sentros."

Barva smiled at the human. "I will try my very best to make as simple as I possibly can."

They passed the gas cloud with minimal interference and Barva checked the scanners for enemy craft, and then opened the communication banks. "This is Barva," he said. "Leader of the Talokian fleet. Prepare stolen Tolarion fleet for the first advancement on Tolaria. After that, the Varcon will advance, and then the Talokian fleet. After we've deactivated their force field, then the Republic will follow."

After the force field was eliminated, the Rebuplic's forces were to meet the Talokians and attack with a full invasion force. At Sentros, another battle was fought and the advance weaponry of the planet overcame the Tolarion forces as they began to retreat. Even though the Tolarions outnumbered the Republic; their weapons technology was inadequate to defeat them all through the galaxy.

This news, which was reported back to Akros, infuriated him to no end. That was the main reason he wanted to see Riona and get him to install the ray gun. The two renegades were directed into the hall, and Akros rose from his chair. "So these are our troublemakers," Akros announced, walking over to them and carefully looked them over, examining Jeff's bruises and bleeding. "I was expecting much more worthy adversaries. Balta, didn't I tell you not to harm him until he saw me first! Can't either of you follow my orders correctly?"

"They would not come willingly," Balta lied. "My men did what they had to, as I did what I had to."

"He's no good to me if you if you half kill him first," Akros said, and stared into Jeff's eyes.

Jeff stared back into his brown eyes with an evil stare. "I know who you are," he exclaimed.

"Oh," Akros said as he smiled. "And who am I?"

"You're Dr. Louis Avery. You worked for NASA about a century ago," Jeff told him.

"You're well educated," Akros answered. "And your name is-"

"Walker," Jeff answered. "Major Jeff Walker. You knew my grandfather, Colonel Thomas J. Walker."

"Yes, of course," Akros recollected another time and place. It was a time when he was not so angry with the human race. "Tom Walker. He was a good man. Not very intelligent, but a good man."

"What's happened to you?" Jeff asked. "You used to be so protective of the human race."

"That was before they laughed at me for my theories, and condemned my research. They took away everything I fought so hard for! As usual, they were wrong!"

"Is that any reason to cause an interstellar war?" Zarcon asked.

Riona pointed his laser at the insect's head. "Can't we just kill them now?" he insisted.

"Not yet," Akros said. "They want any answer, and they're entitled to one. When I left Earth, I was dying. I knew my theories were right, but no one believed me. I was given a vision, in a dream, and the answer was all too clear to me. When I heard that there was a launch to develop a base on Mars, I hijacked the vessel that I had developed with NASA and left to test my theory. I harnessed the power of our sun, and tested this theory over and over again until I discovered how to create a wormhole in space, allowing me to travel anywhere in any universe. When I passed through to this universe and came here, a simple alien virus changed my genetic structure somehow. I began genetic research in hopes that I may become human again, but lacked human subjects for my experiments. This planet was my only refuge.

124

I found this planet had its advantages. The alien organism actually allowed me to live fifty years longer than I expected, and gave me two lung systems, giving me the ability to breathe both Oxygen and Nitrous Oxide. I had a whole world to call my own, and my research flourished. I created every being here using my own two hands!"

"That doesn't explain why you want to destroy everyone," Zarcon replied. "You're a scientist; surely you understand the importance of life?"

"Perfect life," he said and smiled. "On a perfect world, free from disease and death. A world where everyone is treated the same. Your race, Mr. Walker, is arrogant, greedy, and savage. Even by your own standards. Mine is clean, efficient-"

"Conquerous, murdering, malicious," Jeff interrupted. "Your race has already destroyed at least three civilizations!"

"At least they haven't destroyed themselves," Akros argued. "Like so many Earth civilizations of the past!"

"How can you even still call yourself human?" Jeff asked.

"Who ever said I was human?" he answered. "I'm even better! I'm eternal!"

"You were eternal," Riona said, as he quickly drew his laser and pointed at Akros. Akros was bewildered by his behavior.

"Riona?" he yelled, and backed towards the enormous window behind him, overlooking outside the base. "Have you gone mad? Balta, have the guards seize him!"

"They won't follow your orders anymore," Balta grinned and told him. "I'm in command now!"

"So much for your perfect world," Jeff joked, as he and Zarcon remained motionless.

"Silence!" Balta screamed and pointed his laser at the human. "You're next!"

"Please Riona," Akros pleaded. "I've created all of you!" The humanoid edged closer to him, his gun still aimed at him.

"We don't need you," Riona snarled. "We know now how to create our own race! Look at him grovel, the great, powerful Akros!"

"No," Akros persisted. "You can't do this! You need me to guide you! What about the Triachilite?"

"No I don't," Riona said. "I have all the Triachilite I need!"

"Please don't kill me," he said, and put his hands together as if to pray. "Give me a chance!"

"You had your chance," Balta said. "Our process is quicker and more efficient. We have no more use for a mere human!"

"But I created you," he continued.

And I'm un-creating you," Riona jested, as he fired the laser which created a blast that sent Akros through the window, allowing dust and wind to enter the conference room. Akros fell into the canyon below dead. Nitrous Oxide and wind poured into the room. Zarcon and Jeff had to move quickly if they wanted to escape alive.

Jeff, taking advantage of the situation, grabbed Balta around the neck and disarmed him. He pointed the laser at his head until he and Zarcon reached the doorway, and then threw him to the floor. Zarcon quickly took the homing device from his antennae and placed it in his mandibles and swallowed it, as Riona started to go after them.

"Wait," Balta gasped, as he rose from the floor and grabbed his arm. "Set up the fusion ray and set the coordinates on Sentros!"

"But they're getting away," Riona yelled.

"I'll go after them! You just get the gun ready, understand?"

He followed his orders, and headed to the landing bay area where the ray gun was unloaded earlier. It was transported to the main control area to where it was to be operated from. Carrying a laser, Balta proceeded to search for the prisoners. He wanted to make sure they were dead for certain this time. He walked down the corridor, where he met with one of his men. "There are unidentified alien ships entering the atmosphere," his subordinate told him.

"You're kidding!"

"Sir, I wish I was. The force field has somehow been deactivated from inside the complex."

"Zarcon," Balta hissed, as he realized his prisoners again had gotten the upper hand. "Very well. Place all of our troops on alert near the landing bay area. Seal the main control center off and don't let anyone enter it, except for Riona! He knows what to do. I've got some unfinished business to take care of!"

Meanwhile, Jeff and Zarcon had deactivated the base's force field and successfully made it to the laboratory in which the Triachilite was produced. The human kept guard as Zarcon eyed the computer for information on the project.

"This is interesting," Zarcon said, as he glanced at the screen.

"What is it?" Jeff asked.

"According to this, they haven't produced any Triachilite here, only the antidote," the belorion stated. "It must be Riona was supposed to supply the formula."

"It figures," the human remarked. "Does it say where he got it from?"

"Hang on, I'll find out." He punched in the necessary data on the keys, and an array of information was displayed. "He received it on Zacharas, which is in the Tallman star system. Hey, wait a minute, that's where my people are from!"

"That explains a lot of things! Just who is Riona really anyway?"

"I'll see if the Tolarions have a profile on him," Zarcon said, typing in more input. In a matter of minutes, the following information appeared: Riona- A humanoid from Tios Four, star system 8981083. Birth date unknown, joined the Republic in 120, joined Tolaria as double agent in year 124, advanced to Federation Leader in 133, successful takeover of Rotar in 135, takeover of Zeloria in 136, takeover of Beloria in 138, destruction of Zeloria in 138. Level four intelligence expert, extremely dangerous and well trained.

"Jeff, look at this," he said, and gestured for him to look at the screen. The human read it over carefully.

"It appears our Tolarion spy has been very busy," Jeff said. "It doesn't mention how he got the drug, however."

"Perhaps if we give him the antidote," Zarcon suggested. "We can put an end to all of this."

"Yea," Jeff said. "What and where is it?"

"Its called Varibolin," the insect said. "It might be on the table over there." He pointed to a table by the wall. Jeff walked over to it and gazed at the many different colored flasks in front of him.

"Which one?" he asked.

"According to its properties, it appears to be the greenish liquid there."

"Found it," Jeff said, grabbing the flask. "How is it supposed to be administered?"

"Through the skin using a needle." Jeff poured its contents into two syringe bottles, being careful not to spill any. He then gave one to Zarcon, and kept one for himself.

"If you can hold Riona down or keep him occupied," Jeff suggested. "I can inject him with the serum."

"We may not have to worry about that," Zarcon said. "I sensed before that his power was weakening considerably. He needs another injection to sustain it. Perhaps his current supply is running out."

"Well, we can't take any chances," Jeff said. "The fleet is on their way. We have to find him and stop him before they get here."

"What about Balta?" Zarcon asked, as Jeff placed his syringe inside the pocket of his tattered spacesuit.

"He's my problem," the human answered. "First we have to find the ray gun and destroy it."

"Agreed," the insect said, as he put the syringe in his utility belt upon leaving the laboratory.

They edged down a corridor that lead towards the landing bay area and control area, careful to make sure there no guards were about. The area was dead quiet, for most of the Tolarions were engaged in battle or looking for the two escapees.

They came closer to their destination when two guards began to open fire on them. Jeff fired back, and hit one square in the chest. The other attacked Zarcon, swinging at his large head with his fist. Four arms proved to be to his advantage as he grabbed his foe's arms and pierced his lower claws through his victim's chest. He fell to the floor in a pool of blood. They then continued up a stairway to a catwalk which overlooked the main control area. On the catwalk they saw Riona setting up the doomsday device. "There he is," whispered Jeff.

"We're too late," replied Zarcon, as they watched him inject a needle into his pale skinned arm.

"Not yet," Jeff said, and prepared to fire his laser at him.

"I wouldn't do that if I were you," snarled a voice from behind. Jeff turned to face Balta, who was holding a laser at him. Jeff and Zarcon dropped their lasers to the floor. "Our operations are complete. We're getting what we wanted from the beginning-to destroy your precious Republic."

"I've heard of being overly optimistic," Jeff replied. "But what makes you so sure that you've won?"

"It doesn't matter if we've won," the sadistic simian answered. "The destruction of all of your planets is justification enough! In a matter of minutes, President Zarcon, your council's headquarters will explode like a supernova, and there's nothing you can do to stop it! Start it up, Riona!"

Balta turned to his comrade, and as he did, Jeff quickly kicked the laser from his hand. Riona activated the death ray and the fusion reactor started to warm up. "Stop him," Jeff yelled to Zarcon, as he tossed him the other syringe. Jeff swung violently and hit Balta's head, which made him fall to the floor. The Tolarion grabbed his leg, also pulling him to the floor.

Balta scrambled to grab the laser and get on top of Jeff, but Jeff knocked it over the catwalk. Balta jumped on him and struck his face repeatedly thus drawing blood. The human threw him off, kicking him in the side. He then punched him several times until he had the beast against the railing, overlooking a thirty feet drop. He held his arm at the beast's throat. "I never asked for any of this," he hissed. "You brought this upon yourselves!" Balta pushed Jeff away and he fell against the wall.

"Can't you see that you are inferior to me?" Balta preached, as he kicked the human in the stomach. Jeff didn't have much fight left, as both of his eyes began to swell, and blood was dripping from his mouth. When he tried to rise, the Tolarion kicked his face and he fell to the floor, and was dragged to the railing.

He threw Jeff over the catwalk and the human was barely able to grab the railing. Balta grabbed his wrist, trying to make him lose his grip. "Time to die, Mr. Walker," he laughed as the human could no longer hold the rail. Just before the Tolarion was about to let go, he ripped off his mask and was able to grab the knife from Balta's belt. Balta began to gasp, and with his free arm, Jeff threw it into his chest. Jeff grabbed the floor of the catwalk, even to his own amazement.

He lifted himself up, as Balta proceeded to pull the knife out of his body armor, and scrambled to grab his mask, gasping. Jeff pulled his leg and he fell against the catwalk. When Balta's knife was back in his right hand, he turned towards Jeff. "Now I'm going to really get you," he snarled, as he sliced the human's left arm. Jeff jumped away, grabbing his throbbing bloody arm, his pain only secondary to his rage at that point. He was getting tired of this alien, and wanted to end it. He quickly snatched the knife from his foe with his right hand, and kicked him in the stomach. He jumped on him, ripped his mask off again, and punched his face wildly until he was unconscious. He then rose from the floor to help his arthropod companion, but ended up collapsing beside Balta, unconscious himself.

During this time, Zarcon had reached Riona below. "Zarcon," he replied. "You're just in time to watch me destroy that subservient alliance of yours."

"I know the secret of your power," the insect announced, as he held a laser on his nemesis. "It was an ancient drug used by my people many centuries ago. But like any other drug, however, it can be neutralized."

"Why don't you neutralize me then?" the humanoid suggested.

Zarcon pulled the syringe from his belt, as Riona tried to control his arm, but found it difficult to do so. He used his mind to make the insect drop the laser, and watched as Zarcon began to point the needle back towards himself. Zarcon used his lower arm to inject the other syringe into Riona's arm as he screamed in pain, ripping it from his bleeding arm. "You're going to pay for this," Riona yelled and grabbed for the laser, pointing it at the insect.

"Now," he scoured. "Your precious Sentros will be obliterated!"

He reached across the panel and tried to set the coordinates, but Zarcon grabbed his arm holding the laser. He grabbed Riona by the neck with his other arm, and used his two free arms to initiate the self destruct sequence. "No," Riona cried. "Don't you realize what you've done?"

Zarcon threw the laser against the control room wall. "Yes," he said. "I've destroyed your doomsday weapon! And now that you are no better than any other being, let's see how you really can fight!"

He grabbed Riona using all four arms and hurled him across the control room floor. He fell about ten feet away, scrambling for his weapon. Zarcon kicked it away, grabbed and lifted him by the neck, shoving his head against the computer panel. Zarcon spoke to him as he threw him against another panel.

"You are nothing without your Triachilite," he told him. "For years, I respected you as a great leader. I used to be afraid of you, and to this day I don't know why. You're nothing but a disgusting, pathetic, egotistical maniac. I should kill you right now!

"Do it then," he pleaded. "Kill me! It doesn't matter! The destruction countdown has begun! You'll never escape in time!"

"I can't kill you," Zarcon detested. "That wouldn't make me any better than your destructive race!"

There was an explosion and the main door opened. "Zarcon," a voice yelled, as the smoke cleared. His friends entered with a small troop of soldiers, some human and some Talokian. As the insect turned towards them, Riona quickly grabbed the laser and fired it into the insect's back. He fell to the floor in pain and the soldiers opened fire on the humanoid, killing him in just seconds. His laser blasted body fell to the floor.

Dormiton and Milgic ran over to their friend, followed by Carver and Lori.

"Zarcon," Dormiton cried, and raised his friend's head from the floor. The Lingworts wept over their friend. "You can't die!"

129

"Use your thought transference," Milgic suggested with tears in his eyes.

"I cannot," Zarcon said as he gasped for air. His chest was bleeding badly.

"I don't have the energy. Get everyone out of here. The fusion gun is going to self destruct in ten minutes!"

"Barva," John said into his hand held communication device. "Never mind shutting down systems, I repeat abort mission! Evacuate, I repeat, evacuate! This place is going to blow in ten minutes!"

"We read you loud and clear," Barva answered. "Preparing to move out!"

"What about Jeff?" Lori asked, searching the control room.

"Catwalk," Zarcon gasped. He grew weaker with each breath, as he continued to bleed internally.

"Catwalk?" Dormiton asked, as he sobbed over his friend.

"I think he means Jeff is on the catwalk," Carver said, as Lori immediately ran up to retrieve him. She climbed up the ladder, and saw him lying on the floor. She knelt over him, turned his limp body around, and lifted his head.

"Jeff," she said, as he awoke. She wrapped a tourniquet around his arm and tried to stop the bleeding.

"Is that you?" he asked, smiling. "Or am I dreaming?"

"Yea, it's me," Lori answered.

"But how?" he asked. "How did you find me?"

"With a little help from your friends," she said. "They're the ones who brought us here. It's a long story. When we got time, I'll tell it to you."

"I got a feeling I know how it ends," he said, as she helped him to his feet. "Is Balta dead?"

"Balta?" Lori asked, bewildered.

"Yes," he said. "I left him lying next to-" As he turned, he could see that the evasive Balta once again managed to escape. However, without an army or ray gun, he didn't pose a threat at the moment. Lori helped him down the catwalk to where the rest of them where, and walked over to Zarcon.

"What happened?" the weary Major Walker asked.

"Riona shot him," Dormiton stated.

"But not before he accomplished the mission," Carver added.

"Hello John," Jeff said, happy to see another friend's face. He gave him a firm though tired handshake. "Long time no see."

"Yes," Carver answered, and placed his right hand on his left shoulder. "You better speak with your friend. He's dying."

"Isn't there anything we can do for him?" Milgic pleaded.

"I'm afraid not," Lori remarked, as Jeff bent over the insect.

"We did it," he told Zarcon, as he grabbed his claw.

"Yes, we did," Zarcon whispered. "At least I was able to destroy the ray gun. You better go, before it's too late."

"Farewell, Friend," Jeff said, and grabbed his claw tightly. "I'll never forget you."

"And I'll never forget you, Jeff Walker," he answered, closing his eyes for the last time. Jeff's head fell on his chest and he began to weep, removing Zarcon's headband, and gripping it tightly.

"Goodbye, Friend," he repeated over several times. His two lingwort friends tried to pull him away from their companion.

"We have to get out of here now," Carver commanded, as he grabbed Jeff's arm himself. He watched Zarcon and the remains of Riona as he was dragged from the main control center towards the landing bay. He placed the headband in the pocket of his tattered and torn spacesuit.

"Five minutes and counting," the computerized voice announced as they ran into the hangar deck.

They boarded the Varcon immediately, greeted by Barva. As the five passengers boarded, Barva looked out the main door hatch, and the other troops boarded two other ships. "Where's Zarcon?" he asked.

"He's not coming," Carver said, as he climbed in, bowed his head and closed the hatch. Carver glanced towards him as Barva knew in his mind what happened to their friend. "Get us out of here as fast as you can!" Barva nodded, accelerating the vehicle out of the hangar bay and up into the atmosphere.

The fleet of spaceships rapidly emerged from the Tolarion ground base. Destroying Tolaria probably wouldn't mean the end of their arrogant race, but it would mean an end of their tyranny. They watched the exploding planet which looked like a small sun for a moment, as the fusion weapon set off a chain reaction that incinerated the surface of it. They quickly left the solar system and into the darkness. They had successfully destroyed their enemies and restored peace for both universes, and even though Jeff found himself an interesting circle of friends, he couldn't help but feel sorrow for the loss of his friend. Zarcon helped them when they needed it the most; a perfect stranger who turned against his own beliefs to do so. That was the making of a true friend.

Two weeks later, they arrived at the council once again to face Balar. Sentros successfully warded off their attackers, and was ready to greet their heroes with honors. "Where is Zarcon?" he asked, as they entered the chambers.

Jeff stepped up to the table, his arm in a sling. He bowed his head as he explained. "He was killed by Riona," he informed them. "He gave his life to protect this planet and destroy the death ray."

"We are sorry we ever doubted him," Balar said, regrettably. "He has proven to be a great asset. "Therefore, we will award each of you with our medal for bravery." He reached inside a case that was near the table. He placed four medals on the table, and began to hand one to Jeff.

He became a little annoyed by their nonchalant attitude. "Keep your medals," Jeff muttered. "What we really need is a place to live. Balta saw to it that Mars was destroyed. We have no home to go back to."

"I'm sorry to hear that," he said. "You are welcome to live here or perhaps we could find a world to restart your races. If you could live anywhere in this galaxy, where would you like to live?"

The human thought for a minute, looked at the two lingworts, then Lori and smiled. "Ventros," Jeff stated, and the two lingworts and Lori hugged him.

"What's Ventros like?" she asked, gazing into his brown eyes with wonder.

"It's like Earth, Lori," he said. "We're going home to a quiet and peaceful Earth." She smiled, always wondering what Earth looked like. The party walked to the entrance of the council chambers, where they were greeted by Carver and Barva. "And where are you going, Barva?" Jeff asked his genetically connected friend.

"Back to my own people," he said. "Jalok needs me to help our race rebuild itself. We owe it all to you, you know. Perhaps in one hundred years we can help your races reach the peace it took us millions of years for us to achieve."

"Perhaps," Jeff said, and held his hand out to him. Barva grabbed it tightly. "There is one thing you were wrong about though. Humans are more capable than you think of advancement. Akros claims he was creator of the inter-dimensional device. It's too bad that he didn't use it for useful purposes however. Anyway, take care, Friend. If you're ever in the neighborhood, stop by."

"I will," he said. "I still don't totally believe Mr. Akros came up with the idea himself, but it's a mute point now anyway. Take care, Jeff. As an old earth saying goes, I'd like to say it's been fun, but it hasn't."

"I know what you mean," Jeff laughed. "Goodbye, Barva."

"Goodbye, Jeff," he answered as they hugged each other.

Two more weeks passed since their departure from Sentros, and they finally reached home again. Lori and Jeff became closer than they ever were before, and were finally together the way they always wanted to be. The war, although it was catastrophic, brought them together in a way stronger than the bonds of space and time itself. John Carver brought most of the humans to Ventros as well using a fleet of Republic ships with advisors to help them rebuild. They colonized on several small islands within the region of the lingwort's, and other humans remained on Sentros. The lingworts on the other island were transferred to where they wanted to be in the first place. Some of the humans also stayed there to help the lingworts rebuild their small community. They built a new village and named it "Sarrala", which meant 'freedom forever and for all', and started to learn trade with the humans on the other islands.

Jeff and Lori chose to live the primitive life on the island without technological advancements; other than a trusty laser or two. Jeff had enough of it for a while, and wondered why he ever longed for it to return. He was relieved he could return to the days of fishing and cooking on an open fire.

Three months since the Tolarian invasion, Lori and Jeff were walking on the far side of the island. They were catching up on all times, and enjoyed each other's company. They walked through the lush jungle path which led up to the ridge where the base had once been, and he told her of the struggle to save their world. While his back was turned towards the path, a dark figure emerged from the jungle. From behind he felt a thud against the back of his head, and he fell to the ground in pain. He became dizzy, and he faintly made out who it was, as Lori screamed and struggled to get away.

When he regained his senses, he saw that he was struck with a log, and that Lori was fighting off her attacker and was being pushed towards the ledge just above them. Jeff jumped to his feet, and ran up to save his love. He approached, and his attacker turned towards him laughing. "You!" Jeff sneered in anger. He just couldn't seem to kill this monster.

"Yes, Mr. Walker, it is me," his Tolarion nemesis said.

"You're a tough ape man to kill," Jeff told him.

"As you are as well, Mr. Walker." He grabbed Lori's neck tighter as she struggled.

"At least I don't hide behind a woman."

"You're games are starting to bore me," he said, as he pushed her closer to the edge. "I'm going to take away everything you ever cared about, starting with her!"

As he began to throw Lori over the cliff, Jeff reached for her, unable to grab her arm. She grabbed onto a branch just below them to stop from falling, as Balta kicked Jeff in the side. Jeff fell, and Balta kicked him in the stomach several times. "When are you humans going to learn," he said, as he walked back to finish what he set out to do. "You're inferior to us!"

Jeff rose from the ground to face his enemy one last time. He went to push Balta, and he stopped his arm, twisting it. "Give it up," he said. Jeff swung quick with his right hand and hit him right in the face two or three times until he fell. As Balta struggled to pick himself up, Jeff backed up.

"Here's what I think about your superior race!" he said as he took a running kick, powerful enough to propel the Tolarion off the cliff and into the ocean below. While he fell, Jeff watched him, amazed that he didn't even scream and was laughing instead. Jeff reached down to grab the hysterical Lori. She crawled back up to him and embraced him in her arms, crying. "It's gonna be all right," he said. "It's over!"

As the sun set behind them on the tropical island, they were truly thankful for all this experience taught them, and how fortunate they really were to live anywhere in a universe without such turmoil. The most important thing to them was that they had their own Garden of Eden to reshape, and it was for them to decide if they were going to follow good over evil.

ABOUT THE AUTHOR

Nicholas T. Davis lives in East Syracuse, NY, and has been writing since he was 12 years old, was motivated by his seventh grade teacher. He has been married to his wife, Nancy, for 12 years, and has a daughter, Kelly, from a previous marriage. His father was a protestant minister and maintenance worker for Syracuse University and his mother was a homemaker, and he is one of eight children.

He has worked as a cleaner for a psychiatric hospital for 26 years and writes in his spare time. He also oil paints, and is a part time musician. Dimension Lapse is his first science fiction novel. For more information on what his next project will be, please visit his blog or Facebook page.

WHERE TO FIND NICHOLAS DAVIS

BLOG: https://ntdavis18dotcom.wordpress.com

FACEBOOK: **https://www.facebook.com/NATNIGHT**

EMAIL: **ntdavis18@verizon.net**

WATTPAD: **https://wattpad.com/NicholasTDavis**

TWITTER: Nicholas T. Davis@NICKTDAVIS18

LINKED IN: **www.linkedin.com/pub/nicholas-davis/95/b9a/771**